MW01124415

Old Habits
Albert Smith's Mystery Thrillers Book 1
Steve Higgs

Text Copyright © 2024 Steve Higgs

Publisher: Steve Higgs

The right of Steve Higgs to be identified as author of the Work has been asserted by him in accordance with the Copyright, Designs and Patents Act 1988

All rights reserved.

The book is copyright material and must not be copied, reproduced, transferred, distributed, leased, licensed or publicly performed or used in any way except as specifically permitted in writing by the publishers, as allowed under the terms and conditions under which it was purchased or as strictly permitted by applicable copyright law. Any unauthorised distribution or use of this text may be a direct infringement of the author's and publisher's rights and those responsible may be liable in law accordingly.

'Old Habits' is a work of fiction. Names, characters, businesses, organisations, places, events, and incidents either are the product of the author's imagination or are used fictitiously. Any resemblance to actual persons, living, dead or undead, events or locations is entirely coincidental.

Contents

Prologue

He had always known it could happen; he just never thought it would. In the early years, Dirk De Graaf found a constant need to look over his shoulder even if it was only metaphorically. However, the sense that someone might know, that someone might suspect, passed after a time and he learned to relax.

He married, which was a risk in itself – a wife would ask questions about his past, which was only natural, yet it proved simple enough to navigate what he at first perceived to be turbulent waters. It turned out he was a better liar than even he believed.

More than two decades after the lie began, he could not recall the last time he had felt exposed. It had been years for certain, yet today his sense of security crashed to the ground around his feet and in the blink of an eye he saw his past coming at him like a freight train.

The change was brought about by a chance encounter, the kind of event a person can do nothing to protect against. In many ways it was the best-case scenario, for while it felt like there were sharks circling his canoe, it was just one man.

One old man.

And one old man could be dealt with easily enough.

He wanted to check there was no further danger and almost had twice since the encounter. He could do it with one phone call. If the person who answered knew nothing, he would be safe to relax. He wouldn't do so, not for a while at least and his rational side would argue that the danger had been managed.

His hand twitched, reaching for his phone only to stop before it got there. He could make a call, it would only take a moment, but doing so would give life to the paranoia teasing at the edge of his mind. And it wouldn't get him an answer either. Not straight away.

They might double their efforts or recheck the feed from the wiretap to be doubly sure, but that would take time and he would worry from the moment he made the call to the second he heard back.

He withdrew his hand. Not making the call was a lot like sticking his head in the sand like an ostrich, yet he chose to do it, nevertheless.

Angry with his lack of decisive thinking – a personal quality he prided himself on – he rose from his chair and paced to the brandy decanter in the corner of his office. With a large helping warming in the glass in his hand, he looked out across Antwerp.

His office occupied the corner plot on the top floor of an executive office building overlooking Grote Markt, the central square of the city. He was successful in all things, a gift he gave himself through the simple strategy of ruthlessly taking that which he wanted.

It had almost backfired the first time, and might have landed him in jail had fate not provided him a way to cheat the investigating team on his trail. It was yet another reason why he was so determined to eliminate the exposure he now felt. He wouldn't sleep tonight unless he knew it was done.

Mercifully, the task was already in hand. The old man was easy enough to find, easy enough if one had the right contacts. Dirk's local men were on the job, and he would be far from the first person they had been tasked to make disappear.

It would look like a robbery, a mugging gone wrong, an unfortunate incident involving a tourist in the wrong place at the wrong time.

Chapter I

The tram came to a stop, the motion smooth instead of jerky as one might expect on a train. Albert hadn't used trams very often in his life; there were none where he lived in the southeast corner of England. Heck, there were hardly even buses now, he mused, the public transport of his youth fading away with a whimper as everyone became more affluent and cars more prevalent.

With a pneumatic wheeze the doors swung open, exposing all inside to the cold December air which swept in around their ankles, hands, and faces as though hungry for the warmth it might find there.

Absentmindedly, Albert watched the people getting off and ruffled the fur around Rex's neck when new passengers started to get on.

"I fear we may have to shuffle over," Albert warned, his dog looking up at the sound of his human's voice.

Rex leaned out to get a better look, not because he heard what his human said, but because some of the people getting on were carrying or eating food and he was getting hungry. Oversized for a German Shepherd, he had trained and qualified as a police dog with London's Metropolitan Police before being dismissed as impossible to work with. Shortly thereafter he came to live with the old man who now sat at his side and had been his constant companion ever since.

The tram was filling up, the time of day dictating that people were finishing their jobs and heading home. Albert, however, was a long way from his house in England and hoping the tram he was on would deliver him back to his accommodation. It was his first time in Antwerp and undoubtedly his last. Not because he found the city repulsive or was having a terrible time, but due to the simple fact that there were so many other places to go and his years in which to galivant around the globe were limited.

At seventy-eight Albert accepted that he was getting what many would call 'a little long in the tooth'. In his head he was still young and thought of himself as sprightly. He wasn't about to win an athletic competition unless he was pitted against people his own age, but he was a long way from feeling decrepit.

For many years he had served as a police detective, rising through the ranks to reach detective superintendent before his inevitable retirement. It was due to his time spent observing people that he noticed the two men watching the man approaching the empty seat to his right. With so few seats left available, it was inevitable that someone would choose to squeeze in next to him and the dog.

Most had passed by, opting to avoid the chance of slobber or dog hair, but heading right for Albert was a man in his eighties. His pure white hair was thinning and cut short around the back and sides. He had kindly eyes looking out from behind silver framed spectacles and a green and orange silk cravat poking out through the vee where his coat met his neck. He was short at maybe five feet and seven inches, though undoubtedly taller fifty years ago.

It was obvious he intended to ask Albert to shuffle over, so pre-empting the move, Albert gripped Rex's lead tight and stood up. The gap between the rows of seats was such that Albert couldn't sit with Rex between his legs or even next to them without spilling into the space intended for another passenger. Better then that he place Rex in the aisle where he would have a little more room. It was that or put him on his lap and Albert didn't fancy that at all.

"Merci," the man thanked Albert as he slipped by and into the window seat. Albert detected an accent in the single word that set him apart from the other Belgians he encountered since arriving the previous afternoon. He thought nothing of it though. Antwerp, like many European cities, is a melting pot of tourists and workers from across the continent. In all likelihood there were more than a dozen different nationalities represented in the tram's passengers.

Albert guessed the man had chosen to express his gratitude in French because on balance there were as many French speakers as Dutch in Belgium and because more people globally would recognise the French version of 'Thank you'. Equally, he could have opted for English, which most of the population speak due to the international nature of the city and its business.

Resettling in his chair, Albert refocused on the two men. Positioned in the front half of the carriage, Albert had to lean a little to his right, and then his left, to peer around other passengers blocking his view. They were in their thirties, the tall one a few years older than his partner. Standing a shade over six feet, his brown hair was buzzed short all over. A blue tattoo, the design of which Albert could not make out, poked out from the collar of his black hooded top which he wore with a crimson gilet over the top for added warmth. There were tattoos on his hands as well, and probably more beneath his layers of clothing.

The shorter man was five feet and nine inches – Albert got good at judging heights as a police detective. His hair was longer, and bleached blonde though it had grown out so a solid inch of brown showed through underneath. He had no tattoos that Albert could see, but a small scar bisected his right eyebrow. He wore dark blue jeans, box fresh white running shoes, and a winter coat that fell almost to his knees.

They were both Caucasian and in need of some sun to give colour to their pale skin. More than anything they looked like bruisers, the kind of men one employs as a silent threat and then an active solution when the silent threat fails to get the message across.

They came onto the tram through the front door, not the centre one the man now sitting next to Albert used, and had been watching him quite intently to see where he went. They continued to look his way now, checking now and then and each time the tram stopped.

Were they checking to see if he was getting off?

Rex closed his eyes and placed his chin on Albert's thigh. He went where the old man went; his constant shadow. They travelled a lot which he thoroughly enjoyed, not that he really understood the concept. What Rex knew was that every few days they went somewhere new. At each place they stopped he would find new smells to sample and new people to meet. Often as not they ended up getting into some kind of adventure and that made their travels all the more interesting.

The tram continued on its way, wending through Antwerp's streets. It was past closing time for many businesses and just starting to get busy for the restaurants and bars that would service the population until after midnight.

Albert's stomach rumbled, reminding him it was time to feed Rex and thereafter find a place to eat himself. There was a small Italian place he'd walked by the previous evening. Close to his hotel, the smells wafting from it had made him wish to explore its menu even though he was in Belgium and supposed to be sampling the local fare.

The tram began to slow once more and the man to Albert's right gripped the top rail of the seat in front and shifted his knees to face outward; using body language to indicate his intention to alight. Albert saw he was trying to catch his eye and started to rise from his own seat, but Albert's attention was back on the two men in the front half of the bus. They were not looking his way, their focus on nothing much at all now.

The man next to Albert slid out of their row and with the tram still moving, used the upright poles lining the central aisle to support himself on his way to the door.

Albert sunk back into his chair. The two men at the front were talking, chatting about something in a distracted fashion that made Albert laugh at his paranoia. They hadn't been watching the man with the white hair at all. In all likelihood they had been checking out an attractive woman sitting behind Albert.

To satisfy his curiosity as the doors opened and the two men remained where they were, Albert twisted around in his seat to confirm his theory, but found an overweight man chewing gum in an ugly, mouth-open fashion in the seat behind. Next to him was a mousey woman half his size and beyond them Albert could not find anyone who might warrant the two men taking a second look.

The doors swished closed and the tram pulled away. Turning back to face his front, Albert's heart rate spiked, a burst of adrenaline gripping his pulse. The bruisers were gone!

Jumping to his feet, Albert gripped his seat for balance and stared across the tram to see outside. It was dark, but the street outside was illuminated by overhead lights. Fifty yards behind the tram, the old man with the white hair tottered on his way and twenty-five yards behind him the two bruisers followed.

Chapter 2

Cursing under his breath, Albert surged out of his row. He needed to stop the tram, but searching frantically for a bell push – all the buses back home had one so passengers could indicate their desire to get off – he found none.

"Of course there's no bell," Albert growled at himself. He was on a tram, not a bus, and it ran on rails. It couldn't stop just anywhere.

Rex sensed the urgency in his human's steps though he knew not what could have caused it. They were moving toward the front of the tram, Albert excusing himself as he passed between and around those passengers still standing.

Nearing the front, he called to the driver, "I need to get off!"

The driver, hidden behind plexiglass, didn't even turn his head when he muttered, "Next stop is coming up."

Albert gritted his teeth and ducked a little to look back out through the tram's rear window. In the ever-increasing distance, he believed he could still see the old man's white hair meandering along the pavement. However, the street was relatively busy with passing traffic and pedestrians. If the two men were planning anything, and Albert felt certain they were, they would need to wait until their target was somewhere less public and visible.

Moving to the very front of the tram so he could look directly at the driver, Albert shouted, "I need to get off! Someone is about to be attacked!"

The bold and shocking statement made the driver twitch, his eyes leaving the route ahead for a half second so he could take in the crazy old man yelling demands through the plexiglass to his right.

Curling a lip in confusion, the driver said, "Are you threatening me?" He took one hand off the steering wheel to point at a sign mounted on the plexiglass above Albert's head. He couldn't read it, but could guess it advised threatening behaviour would not be tolerated et cetera.

Making his voice deliberately calm and his face placid, Albert repeated, "I need to get off."

Mercifully, the stops were less than five hundred yards apart and the driver was already beginning to slow the tram. Anxiously, Albert ducked again to stare through the back window, but the man with the white hair was now too far away to make out and it came as little relief that he could still see the two bruisers who followed him.

Anyone else might have dismissed Albert's concerns, but he felt sure he knew different. Not that it brought him any pleasure. A lifetime as a police officer and a detective imbued him with an almost sixth sense when it came to spotting criminals. He could not say what the two men might have in mind for their target, yet the certainty of their ill intent drove him to leap from the tram's front doors as they swished open.

The driver shouted something at his back, the comment falling on deaf ears as Albert raced back the way the tram had just come. Not that raced was the best term to employ. Sprightly he might be, but closing in fast on eighty, Albert could run a short burst if necessary, but he wasn't about to cover five hundred yards in a minute or so as he might have done sixty years ago. In fact, he knew with utter certainty that if he attempted to run the whole distance his knees would quit working before he got halfway.

So he walked at his best pace, encouraging Rex to lead with determination.

Rex didn't know where they were going, but the old man's actions and tone told him there was something amiss. Such urgency could mean a person in trouble, but Rex's powerful nose wasn't detecting anything that might give credence to such a concern. There was no blood in the air, no whiff of panicked adrenaline which humans give off in their perspiration. Using his eyes and ears – two lesser senses he employed only when his nose could not get the job done – he could neither see nor hear anything that could give rise to his human's current speed march.

So it was something else, Rex concluded.

Holding his lead, Albert fretted. The two men had vanished from sight in the few seconds it took him to get off the tram. Their disappearance was easily explained; they turned down a side street, but the old man with the white hair was gone too and Albert feared he had been followed into a less populated area – the perfect place for a crime.

In his police career he only happened upon a crime in progress once. It was a mugging which he interrupted purely by chance, the assailant escaping while Albert dealt with the elderly lady victim. She had hit her head when her attacker knocked her down and was bleeding.

He never saw the mugger again; a fact that still angered him because he believed he would have been able to catch the man had he chosen to give chase. How many other victims had he claimed because Albert failed to stop him that night? The memory flashed across his brain, spiking an old sense of rage and injustice.

Hoping he was wrong, but sure he was not, Albert glanced down each side street, searching for any sign of the old man and his would-be attackers. They were past the previous tram stop now, some two hundred yards beyond where the old man got off. The turning he took had to be close by.

Unless he'd already missed it.

The unwelcome voice in the back of Albert's head almost stalled his feet. Would he be able to see them from the main road? Might they have taken yet another turning? Or would the two men have grabbed their victim and dragged him out of sight?

The latter seemed highly likely, but as doubt spread through his body, Albert reached the next side street and his blood froze.

Lying on the pavement a hundred yards down the road, the old man with the white hair wasn't moving. The two men stood over him, and as one moved his arm, a flash of light from an overhead lamp caught on something shiny in his hand: a knife.

Rex's eyes dilated. He could smell human blood. It was fresh and it was close, carried to him by the slight breeze swirling between the parked cars. His hackles rose, but he was yet to work out what was happening when Albert unclipped his collar.

With a slap on his rump to get Rex moving, Albert pointed and yelled, "Sic 'em, Rex!"

It was a command Rex knew well and was happy to obey.

At the sound of Albert's shout, the two men looked up. They needed only half a second to register the danger the German Shepherd posed, and Rex needed only a handful of yards to propel himself from stationary to full sprint. The half second had passed and he was haring down the street toward them with his teeth bared.

Albert got to watch the bruisers make a swift decision. They could have chosen to stand and fight; if one was armed it was likely they both were. Knives against a dog were a good match, but would they be fast enough to stop Rex from sinking his teeth in first? Probably not, and they knew it.

They ran, abandoning their victim without a second glance. They had a good lead on the dog, but his superior speed dictated they could not escape on foot.

Also running, though at a far slower pace, Albert rushed to get to the victim. In the three seconds since he spotted the old man on the ground, he hadn't moved a muscle and Albert feared he might already be too late.

Rex had his head down, his body a fluid blur as his strong legs powered him along the street. Ahead, the men split, the shorter one ducking left between the cars to cross the road, the other carrying on for a few yards before turning right. He shot down an alley, vanishing into the dark shadows thrown by the houses. Knowing he couldn't chase both men, Rex opted for the one still in the street.

Converting his forward motion, Rex bunched his leg muscles to go vertical. Landing on the bonnet of a Peugeot 306, his paws skidded a little on the shiny red paint, but not so much that he couldn't leap down the other side.

His target was twenty yards away; no distance at all. Rex knew he could close the gap in a handful of strides, the man's flailing arms and pumping legs no match for a dog's speed. However, Rex failed to take into account human ingenuity and their willingness to not play by his rules.

Rex had seen, heard, and smelled the pizza delivery man on his moped and were he not engaged in a headlong race to catch a fleeing criminal, he might have salivated at the heavenly scent. What he had not calculated was his quarry's trajectory. When the man he chased ducked through the cars to run across the road, Rex assumed he was just trying to get away.

That was not the case.

Before his eyes, the man swung a meaty arm at the skinny teen as he pulled to a stop. Approaching from behind, the kid never saw it coming.

The open-handed blow struck the backside of his helmet just behind his left ear. It felled him, launching the rider from the moped which might have fallen had the attacker not used his other hand to grab the handlebars.

Rex barked his frustration, his canine brain able to calculate that he was just a fraction too far away to prevent what was about to happen.

The man swung onto the moped and cranked the throttle. It was already pointing in the right direction which allowed Rex's quarry to shoot down the street.

Fifty yards to his rear, Albert huffed and puffed to a stop. His knees were asking questions in a loud and insistent voice and they were not the only part of his body opting to complain. Ignoring it all, Albert had his phone in his hand, the call to emergency services already placed.

Crouching over the still body of the old man with the white hair, Albert felt for a pulse. Truly expecting to find nothing but bad news, he jolted when it thumped beneath his fingers. He was alive, but unconscious, which was a relief. However, a damp patch on the front of the man's coat showed that he'd been stabbed. Albert's hand came away slick with dark red. The wound was right over the victim's heart.

The call to emergency service connected, a voice speaking Dutch, a language Albert could just about recognise. The exact meaning of the words was lost yet he knew the person would be asking him what service he required or what emergency he was calling about. He also knew he could speak in English and be confident the emergency dispatcher would understand every word, but before Albert could respond, the man's eyes snapped open and he grabbed Albert's right wrist.

Staring up with pain-racked eyes, he lifted his head from the pavement.

"It was Kurt Berger!"

Chapter 3

The stab victim blurted the words, the vicelike grip with which he held Albert's wrist and the desperation in his eyes made it undeniably obvious how important he felt it was to give Albert the name of his attacker.

Message given, the old man slumped back to the pavement, his grip loosening as he faded into unconsciousness once more.

Feeling a little bewildered, it took Albert a second to reply to the voice still coming over his phone.

"Yes! Yes. I need the police and an ambulance please. There's been a stabbing."

Rex sprinted after the moped, but he knew within a few strides that he would not be able to catch it. Its top speed wasn't much faster than he could run, but the difference was enough. Angry to have been defeated, he barked his rage into the night and slowed to a stop. The red light on the moped's rear end continued down the street, the man on it glancing back only once to confirm he'd successfully left the dog behind.

Rex knew he could track the exhaust smell, but that was only good for a certain distance. Every vehicle has its own unique smell; a combination of the hydrocarbon mix and whatever else the engine might be burning such as a little engine oil or coolant. It made cars, bikes, and other motor vehicles as unique as a person or a dog, but in a big city the scent would be lost among the other traffic in no time, so Rex reversed course and started to run back the way he came.

The other man had been on foot when he turned into the alley so perhaps it was still possible to catch him.

He ran as fast as he could, but finding the alley when he caught the man's scent and followed it, he didn't get very far before he was defeated again. The alley led to a tall gate that blocked his path. Had it been made from wood or some other solid material, Rex might have considered taking a run up to scale it, but it was constructed of thin steel bars and there was no way to get over it.

Panting from the effort of running and the adrenaline giving chase generated, he nudged the gate with his head to see if it might move. It didn't, and there was no sound to indicate the man was anywhere nearby. Just like his accomplice, he had given Rex the slip.

"*Oi, oi,*" a small voice growled from the darkness behind Rex.

He craned his neck around to find a Jack Russell cross looking at him with its head canted over to one side. He was about to tell it to shoo when his nose locked onto the scents of more than a dozen more dogs.

"*What do we have here?*" asked the Jack Russell cross. The tip of its tail was missing, and its left ear had a tear in it. Its coat was dirty too, but Rex didn't need the visual cues to tell him what his nose already knew: he was looking at a stray.

"*Urgh,*" said a new voice. "*A domesticated.*"

Rex turned his head back to face the gate to find a grubby bichon frise approaching on the other side. There were more dogs appearing from the gloom both in front and behind him.

"*Yes, I cohabit with a human. It is a rewarding endeavour,*" Rex replied. Strays could be trouble if they chose to be and were surprisingly territorial given that they eschewed the concept of a place to live. He had neither the time nor the inclination to tussle with a local pack, either verbally or otherwise, so turned to face back toward the street.

The Jack Russell cross had been joined by an old blood hound whose ears completely covered his eyes, a wiry border terrier thing, and a Pitbull who looked like he could bite through steel. There were more dogs crowding in around him.

Rex didn't want any trouble, but he wasn't going to say that. The strays were all small dogs, attesting to the universal truth that it is harder for a large dog to stay hidden. They wouldn't offer him much opposition if he felt it was necessary to go through them, but the Pitbull ... the Pitbull was a different proposition.

"*I'm going to kindly ask you to step aside,*" Rex delivered his words in a measured manner, making sure to sound calm and unflustered, while also leaving no doubt there was an unspoken 'or else'.

"*Oh, not so fast, Big Boy,*" cooed a voice that bypassed Rex's brain and went straight to his nether regions.

He snapped his head around, or more accurately, it snapped around without instruction to do so. Sauntering up to the gate was a springer spaniel with a sultry gait to her stride. She lifted her nose and sniffed deeply.

"*Hmmm, you smell all kinds of good, gorgeous, but you are not local. I know all the local dogs. In fact, I don't think you are even from Antwerp.*"

Mesmerized, Rex managed to mumble, "*Um, no, I'm travelling. I'm a travelling dog.*"

"*Well, that's almost as good as being a stray,*" the spaniel cooed.

"*No, it isn't,*" argued the Pitbull.

The spaniel narrowed her eyes, the Pitbull choosing to close his mouth and duck his head. Suddenly, the ground beneath his feet proved quite interesting.

"*Never mind him,*" remarked the spaniel who Rex had now identified as the alpha. "*He's always grumpy. Now, you are a long way from home, Big Boy, so what led you into this dark alley?*"

Still finding that his mouth was being controlled by something other than his brain, Rex managed to say, "*I was chasing someone. A man. He came this way.*"

"*Oh, yes, we caught his scent. He ran off, I'm afraid. Was that your human?*"

"*My human?*" Rex repeated the words, his mind a fog of lustful thoughts captured by the spaniel's eyes. He could barely feel his paws, and was losing all notion of time and space when a human voice cut through his consciousness.

"Rex!"

With a snap, Rex's thoughts refocused on Albert, and he ran from the alleyway, sparing one last look at the spaniel before he hit the pavement and lost sight of her.

Returning to the street, Rex spotted his human crouching over the body of the victim and could smell the man's blood on the air. Pushing thoughts of failure from his mind, Rex padded in their direction.

Albert caught movement from the corner of his eye and was relieved to see his dog returning. He'd lost him more than once in recent times, but there had been good cause to give the order to chase. Had he not done so, the two men might have elected to make sure their victim was dead. It seemed like an error to have left him alive.

His wound was grave though and Albert felt the victim's chances were slim at best. The emergency services were on their way, their speed of response likely to determine if the old man lived or died. His age was against him, but his pulse, though weak, was still pumping away in his neck.

Albert had checked for identification but found none. There was no wallet or phone and his watch was missing too, a slight indentation in the skin around his right wrist a telltale sign to show it was there until moments ago.

A mugging then, but why the stab wound? Muggers want petty cash and easily traded goods such as watches, there's no need to invite a murder rap by using a knife when the threat of it should be enough. Or a cosh would do it. A blow to the head to subdue a victim was all the crime warranted.

Albert removed his coat and used it to help keep the victim warm even though it meant he would get cold. The air, a shade above freezing, could be described as frigid. There wasn't a lot of breeze and good thing too for that would have made it twice as bad. Thankfully, he had Rex to hold close and could take some heat from him.

They huddled, Albert constantly checking the victim's pulse until the sound of approaching sirens came close enough to make him rise and wave to be sure they saw his location.

Retrieving his coat when the paramedics raced to give aid, and standing back to give them space, Albert murmured a question that only he would hear, "Who the heck is Kurt Berger?"

Chapter 4

U nsurprisingly, the police asked the exact same question when Albert revealed the man's blurted words. The paramedics wasted little time assessing the victim's condition as critical and were gone with him in the back of their ambulance less than two minutes after arriving. That was all the time it took them to stabilise his blood pressure and get him onto their gurney.

The police had pulled in mere seconds after the paramedics, two squad cars bearing officers in uniform followed by a detective half a minute later.

When he finished interviewing the pizzaboy, who wasn't hurt, but was hopping mad about his moped and sudden inability to earn money, the detective introduced himself as Lieutenant Bervoets. Too senior to have been dispatched to the scene, Albert guessed he must have been on his way home when the call came through - he was passing so he took it.

Bervoets was tall and thin with a nose that angled slightly to the left of his face. It had been broken at some point and never reset. Albert idly wondered if there was a story behind it. In his mid-forties, he wore his sandy brown hair short at the back and sides, though it was overdue a cut, and a side parting on the right – a functional hairstyle that required little effort.

Albert described the attackers with as much detail as he could muster. Their heights, their clothes, their eye colour, and hair styles. Quizzing him at the side of the road a few yards from where the attack took place, Bervoets remarked on Albert's impressive memory as though questioning how he could recall so much detail.

Albert explained his former life as a police detective while silently cursing that he'd not thought to take a photograph. It would have been easy to do on the tram; he could even have pretended to be taking a selfie.

He gave his name and the name and address of the hotel in which he was staying.

The detective's brow creased.

"That's nowhere near here," he remarked, eyeing Albert with a hint of suspicion. "You said you were on a tram with the victim and his attackers. Why would you get off so far from your destination?"

"Because I could see what was going to happen." Albert felt he'd already made this point clear. "The two men were watching the victim too intently."

The frown deepened. "So you chose to alight from the tram and follow them to see whether you were right? It didn't occur to you to call the police before the attack took place?"

"And tell you what?" Albert had to fight not to give a derisive snort. "That I thought an attack might be about to happen? How many stupid calls do the police get in an average day?"

Bervoets acknowledged the point and asked, "What are your movements over the next couple of days, Mr Smith? Do you plan to stay in Antwerp? I believe I may have more questions for you."

Albert sighed and nodded his head; he'd been expecting it. He had told the detective too much, made himself seem too well informed and now he was curious about the how and why even though Albert had supplied a perfectly reasonable explanation already.

"I am leaving tomorrow," he replied, wondering if the detective might now order him to remain in the city.

"And where are you going next, Mr Smith?"

"To La Obrey in France."

One eyebrow rose. "La Obrey?"

"Yes, it's the home of the bretzel. I am interested in food. I came here to sample waffles." Albert was telling the truth ... well, sort of. His trip around Europe was a follow up to a culinary tour upon which he embarked in Britain several months earlier. At the time his interest in learning about famous regional dishes was genuine, now it was more of an excuse.

Whether too bored to question Albert's motivation or simply dismissing him as a potential part of the attack, the detective closed his tablet and put it away.

"Very well, Mr Smith. I have your phone number and you have my card. If you think of anything else, please contact me, but I doubt we will catch them even with your excellent descriptions. There are organised gangs of muggers and thieves in Antwerp much as there are in any major city, in all likelihood after tonight they will move to a new place; easier to avoid getting caught that way."

"Mugging?" Albert repeated. "You're listing this as a mugging?"

The detective had been turning away, keen to get back to his car and out of the cold, but he paused to raise his eyebrows at Albert.

"Of course. This happens all the time, Mr Smith. The victim was well dressed which suggests affluence and he left the tram in De Leine, the city's most expensive postcode."

Albert looked about. He'd noticed the plush houses, fine cars, and clean streets, yet too preoccupied with more pressing matters, had given no thought to what they signified.

Bervoets continued, "Perhaps he wore an expensive watch and they saw it earlier today. Expensive watch could mean a wallet full of cash; older people are more inclined to carry it still, and when he refused to give up what he had they stabbed him. If he comes around I will ask him myself."

Albert wanted to argue, but wasn't sure what to say. Every point the detective raised was valid and his assessment of the likely chain of events could easily be true. Yet it niggled at Albert because something about it all wasn't right.

"The victim named his assailant." Albert delivered the statement just as Bervoets was about to make a second attempt at getting to his car. It wasn't deliberate, just the way Albert's timing fell, but the tightening skin around the lieutenant's eyes suggested he believed otherwise. Regardless, Albert pressed on. "I already told you that. Surely that ought to indicate it was more than a random mugging? Please tell me you have officers investigating Kurt Berger."

The detective nodded at the question. "We have already checked the name, Mr Smith, we can do such things easily these days," his smug reply intended as a dig to Albert's age and how long it had to be since he was actively involved in police work. "There is no one listed by that name in our criminal database and no one called Kurt Berger listed as resident in Antwerp or even Belgium." Giving Albert a kindly smile one might otherwise reserve for the mentally inept, he said, "I'm sorry, Mr Smith, I think it likely that you misheard him."

With a nod to the uniformed cops, who had been liaising with a duo of forensic people taking photographs and checking the area for physical evidence, the detective walked away.

Albert let him go, watching until he got into his car and started the engine. He was about to give Rex's lead a tug; it was time they too went on their way, when an urgent question sent him into the street to stop the car before it could pull away.

"Yes, Mr Smith?" Lieutenant Bervoets remained polite but was doing little to hide the bored irritation in his tone.

"What hospital was the victim taken to, please? I should like to check on him tomorrow and maybe take him something to make his stay easier."

"Universitair Ziekenhuis I should think, Mr Smith. That is the nearest and the best able to handle his surgical needs."

Albert murmured his thanks and stepped back so the detective could leave. Watching the car, a newish Citroen, pull away, Albert turned up his collar; the cold was already creeping into his bones. In his day he liked to think he would have offered an older person such as himself a lift somewhere, especially at this time of the year, but left in the street by himself, he aimed his feet at the main road and hoped it wouldn't be long before the next tram came along.

Perhaps he would check out that little Italian place tonight after all.

Chapter 5

"You're not certain?" Dirk De Graaf was not used to failure. "How can that be?"

Shifting their feet uncomfortably like two naughty schoolboys trapped in front of the headmaster's desk, Jonas Janssens and his partner Matthais Rennier had been working on their story all night.

"I stabbed him in the heart just as instructed," Matthias reported. "But we were interrupted before we could make certain he was dead."

Dirk frowned. "Interrupted by who?"

"By whom," Jonas corrected, instantly regretting it when his employer aimed a scowl his way.

Matthias saved him by saying, "By an old man and his dog. It was a giant German Shepherd and he set it on us. We were lucky to get away. But we know which hospital Erich is in and will go back to finish the job as soon as it is safe to do so. The target did not see us," he added, wanting to get all the plus points across as quickly as possible, "so there is no danger he can give the police a description."

"But the old man with the dog saw you, did he not?" Dirk snapped, angry at their incompetence. They had been useful employees for many years but if there existed a chance that the police could find them, they would need to be eliminated. He would do anything to stop the police ever taking too close a look at his affairs.

Matthias and Jonas exchanged a nervous glance. They *had* been seen, and Jonas really wasn't sure if the pizza delivery boy would be able to give a description. They weren't going to mention him though.

"He was a long way off," Matthias offered.

"A hundred metres maybe," Jonas agreed, exaggerating along with his partner.

Raising a hand to silence them both, Dirk glared through narrowed eyelids.

"Listen up, idiots. I want them both dead, do you understand?"

Jonas opened his mouth to speak, wanting to point out that they had no idea who the man with the dog was, but one look from his employer killed the words while they were still in his mouth.

"I don't care who you have to hurt to find out who got in your way. Kill Erich Jannings and then kill the old man who saw you stab him. Is that clear enough for you two dummies?"

He watched them depart, knowing they would put every effort into doing precisely as he commanded. Dirk De Graaf didn't like loose ends.

Pushing thoughts of Jonas and Matthias from his mind, he returned to what he had been doing, for getting recognised in the street wasn't the only drama currently plaguing his mind.

There was the small matter of Harold De Waele to consider.

He fell into the role of stockbroking more by accident than design. His father drove a bus and his mother worked as a receptionist/accountant for a small lumber firm, hardly the environment one might expect to produce a multi-millionaire businessman. A basic need to escape the blue-collar life he was born into drove him to excel at school and a documentary he caught on TV one day in his mid-teens did the rest.

He set his sights on life as a trader and the hedonistic lifestyle that went with it. There were fortunes to make, and he was greedy. Greedy in a good way, he always told himself, but definitely greedy.

It wasn't fast enough though or, more accurately, he wasn't good enough. He made almost as many bad deals as he made good ones, so when the first firm he worked for chose to let him go, he looked for a way to rig the game.

The industry had a term for it: insider trading, and it was highly illegal. Nevertheless, he made sure to have an unfair advantage and when his cheating led to the biggest windfall of his life, he was hooked.

How could he not be?

However, despite the care he took, an investigator came asking questions. He lied, he made excuses, he made it sound as though the person to be investigated was one of his colleagues. He did it all while sounding concerned and being cooperative. Behind his honest expression his heart had threatened to beat out of his chest and his hands dripped with the sweat of someone who can feel their freedom slipping between their fingers.

The lies would buy him some time, but that was all it did.

Fate chose to give him a way out, a second chance, and when it came, Dirk De Graaf took it with both hands. One moment he was in utter peril, the next he was free as a bird. Free to start it all again, but better.

He was even more careful than before and had layers of security, dummy firms, and other people's names separating him from the truth of his financial activity. On the face of it he was a successful broker, one of the best in the country, but just like his early career, he was rigging the game.

It worked. It worked so well it was hard to believe no one asked how he managed to pick so many winners. In more than two decades there had never been an investigation into his practices, but on top of being recognised as he left his office the previous morning, he had a private investigator asking questions.

It was trouble he didn't need and therefore the situation was shortly to be resolved. Harold De Waele, a former cop, was poking around in a deal that was more than two years old. There hadn't been anything actually illegal about it. Unethical, for sure, but not actually illegal. Nevertheless, if he dug deep enough, it was tenable that he would connect one of the city's most eminent businessmen and philanthropists to the shady deal. Unlikely, perhaps, but not impossible.

Dirk could guess who hired him, but he needed to know for certain and how much he had been able to find out. De Waele wouldn't want to reveal the truth, but he would as soon as he realised the pain wasn't going to stop.

Then the Dutch P.I. would be found in the river, his body unidentifiable.

Chapter 6

Albert's decision to delay sampling the famous Belgian waffles was based on a desire to eat them at what he felt was the right time of the day – breakfast – and the hope that local knowledge might steer him to the best place to get them. Walking from the train station to his accommodation the previous day he passed no fewer than twenty-five places boasting the best waffles in the city and suspected they all offered a perfectly acceptable version of the dish.

However, it wasn't so much the perfect taste he was after but the ambience. The whole package if one will. That meant he needed to eat the famous dish in the best location and to find that he quizzed the hotel staff.

It invited a conflict of opinion, yet they proved unanimous, every person he asked stating that Café Wilte was the place to go. It occupied a prominent position overlooking the River Scheldt and though pricey, it was the only way to enjoy the nation's most iconic dish. Albert worried he would have to book or that they would refuse to let Rex in, but that proved not to be the case, the restaurant staff seating him at a table with floor to ceiling windows overlooking the river. With the sun high and the sky blue despite the cold outside, he had to agree it was a great place to enjoy a meal.

His only wish in that moment was that his late wife could have been there to enjoy it with him. Of course, were it not for Petunia's passing, he would never have seen the need to venture so far from his home. The house they lived in for more than five decades, the house in which they raised three fine children, was thick with her memory. Her voice echoed in the hallways of his mind, making him forget that she was not in the garden or the kitchen; just out of sight, but there if he just called her name.

Her haunting memory, the yearning to wake and find her in the bed by his side drove him from the house many months ago when he first set off to explore the

British Isles with Rex. That trip came to an end, but nothing much had changed. If anything it was worse when he finally returned to their empty house. On the road he could pretend Petunia was at home waiting for his return. No such joy could be found, however fleeting, once he was back inside the echoing loneliness of their four walls.

Forcing thoughts of Petunia from his mind, Albert focused instead on memories of his previous trip. During his culinary adventure around Britain, where he intended to learn to cook some of his favourite dishes and failed miserably, he continually encountered mysteries to solve. As though guided by God's hand, everywhere he went, he arrived just in time to stumble into a crime taking place.

Here in Antwerp it was proving no different.

A yawn split Albert's face just as the waiter approached with his breakfast. He had to hide it with one hand and when it refused to dissipate, used a thumb to offer his thanks.

Sleep had come only after a long period staring at the ceiling the previous evening, Albert's mind swirling with thoughts about the unnamed old man. He knew what he heard the man say and Kurt Berger was a real person whether the police believed it or not. There was a tug at his core to unravel the mystery, which for him was becoming an old habit, but Albert had no need to embroil himself in whatever was behind the attack. In fact, he told himself, it would be foolhardy to do so.

Rex raised his head when he heard his human scraping his cutlery over the plate. At home he provided a trusted crockery cleaning service and could see no reason why that would be any different anywhere else.

Looking up to find the old man looking down, Rex lifted his eyebrows in a hopeful question.

"I saved you a bit," Albert whispered, looking around to check no one was looking his way before easing his plate off the table.

Rex tilted his head sideways, slurping the morsel of waffle and licking the cream with as much speed as he could muster.

Without Petunia to anchor him, Albert was free to go wherever he chose and had a couple of stops planned before returning to England for Christmas. He had grandchildren, and though most were adults now and some were nearly thirty, he still had one granddaughter who would sit on his knee or snuggle under his arm to watch a Christmas movie. He wasn't going to miss out on seeing her for the holiday season.

Despite all the positive thoughts in his mind and the sound knowledge there was no good reason to revisit the incident from last night, Albert needed to know if the victim had survived. Perhaps the abundance of curiosity was what made him such a good detective back when he was a police officer, but whatever it was, Albert knew he was going to continue to want to know who Kurt Berger was until the day he died.

With a sigh, he flagged down a taxi outside the restaurant and asked to be taken to, "University Zebrahorse."

The taxi driver, a woman in her late twenties with short brunette hair and a multitude of earrings in each ear, grinned at his terrible pronunciation.

"Universitair Ziekenhuis?"

"That's the fella. Is it close by?"

"No, not really," the cabbie laughed again. Twisting in her seat she looked Albert up and down. "Are you okay? You're not going to have a heart attack in my taxi, are you?"

Wondering if she might choose to dump him at the kerb if he said, "Yes,' Albert shook his head. "No, I'm fine, thank you. I'm just going to visit a ... friend." He didn't know the man's name or anything about him, but hoped a description of his injuries and the approximate time he arrived would be enough for the hospital staff to find the right person.

The cabbie shrugged her shoulders, flicked on the indicator, and pulled into traffic.

Rex wondered where they were going, but sitting on the backseat with his head up and his tongue out, he contented himself with looking out the window. What they got up to each day tended to be different from the day before and often as not they did it in a new location. Rex didn't much care where they went or what they did because there was always food to eat and usually something fun to do.

Take last night as an example: he got to chase two men and then he ate pasta from his human's plate. Does life get any better?

The hospital soon loomed large in front of the taxi windscreen, the modern building looking like an art gallery or a university as much as anything else. White and angular, it was not what Albert pictured. The sign outside made it clear he was in the right place though, so he handed over some notes, told the cabbie to keep the change, and stepped out onto the street where Rex already waited.

A pigeon cooed from the backrest of a nearby bench and when Rex glanced its way it tilted its head to one side to look back with beady bird eyes. Next to the bench was a bin which Rex liberally 'watered' to show his disdain for the bird.

He wasn't a fan of birds in principle. He didn't like the way they could evade a dog by taking to the air. It was cheating in Rex's eyes, but they were still better than squirrels.

The pigeon continued to coo when he walked away, the unintelligible noises seeming to taunt him.

Inside the hospital a security guard intercepted Albert when he was barely a foot inside the automatic doors.

"I'm sorry, Sir. No dogs allowed in the hospital unless they are assistance dogs."

Albert expected the challenge and was prepared for it. In England he'd snuck his dog into various places but often as not he found Rex wasn't allowed. However, it was suggested to him that he could register Rex as an emotional support animal and that were he to do so, the dog would be able to go more or less everywhere.

Albert not only thought the concept ridiculous, but expected to be rejected when he applied. He needed to be interviewed by a mental health professional to obtain the letter, but after hours of dredging his brain for legitimate reasons why Rex should qualify, he found that he didn't even need to give one.

His application was rubber stamped instantly, not because the process is that easy, but due to the simple fact that Albert Smith was considered by many to be a national treasure. Unwittingly, he'd saved a whole bunch of people held captive by a distant relative of the king and then given them a huge sum of money to help them get back on their feet. The money wasn't exactly his, although the law would state otherwise. It was winnings from a bet he'd mistakenly placed while trying to figure out yet another mystery. So, yes, it was his money, but he had no use for it, and he would never have earned it had he not been on the trail of a murderous royal.

The paperwork satisfied the security guard who escorted him to the reception desk where he asked one of the ladies to issue Albert with a badge.

"Otherwise you will get stopped every two minutes," the guard explained.

Thanking the man for his help, Albert turned his attention back to the lady behind the desk.

"Hello, I'm hoping you can help me to find someone who was admitted last night."

Sixty seconds later and armed with directions, Albert attempted to negotiate the hospital's labyrinth of passages. They were extra wide to allow for orderlies pushing beds and colour coded to boot, yet it still took him three attempts to find the right ward.

The old man with the white hair was listed as Erich Jannings, a fact Albert learned from the helpful woman at the reception desk. She could not tell him how the identification had been made; that information was not shown on her computer, but having a name helped Albert to be sure he had the right place when he arrived at the critical care unit.

Inside the ward's double doors, a nursing station doubled as another reception desk.

A robust woman with greying hair and halfmoon spectacles on a chain looked up to see Albert approach. She looked down at the dog by his side, her lips narrowing in displeasure though she chose not to say whatever she was thinking.

"I'm looking for Erich Jannings," he stated with a warm smile to ward off her frosty expression.

Without looking up from her paperwork, the nurse to her left said, "That's the German tourist from last night."

The frosty nurse said, "Third door on your left," and aimed an arm the way Albert needed to go while muttering something about the ward turning into a doggie day care centre.

Albert had no idea what she meant until he found the right room and the labrador inside it. The dog, a golden-haired bruiser twisted its head around to look at the door when Albert's shadow fell across it, but did not attempt to get up. He was attached to a woman's hand and was quite clearly her guide dog.

Guessing her to be a relative and probably Erich's daughter, Albert recorded her age as somewhere north of fifty. She looked tall even though she was sitting, and her hair was coloured a deep, lustrous brown to hide the grey that ought to be coming through at her age. She wore jeans and shin-height brown leather boots that complemented her sweater. Her outfit, hair, and general appearance suggested she had no trouble paying her bills.

Rex's nose was doing double-time.

"*There's a dog inside,*" he remarked, mostly to himself as he knew for certain his human had no ability to understand him. Snuffling air into his nose to sample the new dog's scent, he concluded, "*Neutered middle-aged female labrador. She lives in a house with a lavender air freshener and is given whole fat milk to drink after her breakfast; it lingers on her breath. She had an encounter with a cat recently and has a small cut that she reopened while scratching.*"

Had Albert been able to translate his dog's odd chuffing noises, he might have said something along the lines of, "Ok, Sherlock, calm down," but just as Rex already knew, he thought his dog was just making sounds. Ignoring them, he knocked on the edge of the door, politely announcing his intention to enter before gripping the door handle to do so.

The labrador rose to her feet and the woman turned toward the door. Her eyelids were half open, the pupils doing nothing to convey the world around her.

"Hallo?" she said in question before Albert could announce himself.

Hearing her accent and recalling that the Erich was German – another fact he learned from the lady at the hospital's main reception desk, Albert replied with, "Guten morgen." Then he got a little lost and figured it was best to stop trying to communicate in the lady's first language. "Um, hello, I'm Albert Smith."

Rex and the labrador were sizing each other up, both at the end of their leads to sniff and check the other out. Rex had been confused about where they were going and hadn't picked up the scent of the old man from the previous evening until his human opened the door.

"*I'm Rex,*" said Rex, wagging his tail. The labrador wasn't displaying any threat signals and smelled friendly enough.

"*Endal,*" the labrador replied. "*You some kind of assistance dog? They don't normally let dogs in the hospital. You're the first I've seen, in fact.*"

Rex didn't know the answer, but said, "*I go where my human goes. Is the man recovering? It smelled like he lost a lot of blood last night.*"

Endal's eyebrows twitched a little. "*It was you, wasn't it? I thought I could smell a trace of another dog on his clothes. What happened to him?*"

"*He was stabbed. I chased off the men who attacked him while my human called for help.*"

"*That's sounds like fun. I never get to do anything like that.*" There was a lament in her tone that suggested Endal wanted a little adventure in her life.

Above the dogs the German woman's eyebrows twitched a little, her face showing that she didn't know the visitor's name and was wondering if she should.

Seeing his error, Albert proceeded to explain, "I apologise for the intrusion. I'm the person who found your father last night." He was about to say that he hoped to see if he was okay and that was why he'd popped by, but the woman had leapt from her chair and was coming for him.

Unable to judge the distance accurately, she reached out with her right hand. Albert met it with his own, but was surprised when she pulled him into a hug.

"Thank you so much, Mr Smith. You are wonderful man." She squeezed him with genuine thanks. "You saved my father's life."

"I was just in the right place at the right time," Albert mumbled, embarrassed. "It was Rex who scared away the men who attacked him. All I did was call for help." Albert knew he was being modest, but the assessment of his role was accurate, nevertheless. It was the swift reaction and skills of the paramedics and doctors that had saved her father's life.

"Nonsense," the woman argued, releasing Albert and stepping back. "I was assured by the surgeon who operated on him that he would not have made it to the hospital had there not been a Good Samaritan to make that call." Reaching out again and bending her knees and waist, she felt for Rex who lifted his head to accept her affections.

"*That's right,*" he panted happily. "*I am the hero of the hour. You may worship me.*"

Endal rolled her eyes.

Cupping his face and feeling his ears, the woman guessed, "He's a shepherd?"

"He is."

"My, he's a big one."

Rex grinned. "*Damned skippy.*"

Straightening, the woman tutted, "Goodness, where are my manners. I haven't introduced myself." She thrust out her right hand. "Franka Schweiger and this is Endal." She patted the labrador's head.

Albert returned her grip. "Albert Smith, but you already knew that. Endal is an unusual name." He used the remark as something to say that wasn't a direct question about her father. He survived, which was good news, yet it was the desire to know more about Kurt Berger that brought him to the hospital, and it was only a sense of decorum that prevented him from diving straight into questions on the subject.

"Yes," she smiled. "She's my be-all and end-all. She does so much for me." Franka replied to Albert's question, but all the while her mind had been working on something that was troubling her. Her face clouded a little, her forehead creasing in thought.

"Albert Smith?" she repeated his name as a question. "That's not the same Albert Smith who ..." She gasped, adding the clues and reaching the right conclusion.

"The one who has been in the news recently?" Albert checked where she was going. "Yes, I'm afraid so. You're going to ask what I am doing here and then remark on how I have a nose for trouble."

"Well, nothing so indelicate, but ... yes, if you can forgive my curiosity."

Albert looked at the two chairs arranged facing the bed. He had a bunch of questions for the lady to answer – her father was rigged to machines and either asleep or unconscious. Whichever it was, he wasn't going to be answering his questions any time soon, so he had to hope Franka would know the name 'Kurt Berger'.

Chapter 7

"No, sorry," she offered a glum face. "That's not a name I am familiar with. Why do you ask?"

Albert sighed. He told the police the name was the last thing Erich said before passing out. Erich felt it was the most important thing he could use his final conscious breath to impart yet clearly Lieutenant Bervoets considered the information to be of no significance. Or simply that it was a red herring. The latter was more likely; Bervoets had not struck Albert as incompetent, but he claimed to have already researched the name and drawn a blank, concluding that Albert misheard or misunderstood what Erich said.

"The police who spoke with you didn't say that name at any point?" Albert's voice came laced with incredulity. Even if the police believed he had misheard the name, surely it was still worth checking.

"No, sorry," Franka apologised again. "Who is he?"

Albert let his shoulder's slump. "I have no idea, but your father clearly did. Your father was unconscious when I found him, but he came round when I started to check his pulse and he said, 'It was Kurt Berger!' in exactly that tone. I think he was naming the man who attacked him."

"Kurt Berger," Franka repeated the name half a dozen times in succession, trying to jog her memory. Tutting, she said, "I'm afraid my father knew a lot of people, but I have to warn you that he is suffering from Alzheimer's. It's early stages and he has more good days than bad, but his memory is getting spotty. It could be that Kurt Berger, whoever that is, has nothing to do with what happened yesterday."

Albert pursed his lips and thought. He could present no argument; there was nothing to base one on, but his gut was screaming at him all the same. The man he met oh so briefly had a clear message to impart. He was naming the man who stabbed him, Albert was willing to wager money on it.

"Have they given any indication when he might wake up?"

Franka shook her head slowly from one side to the other. "Only to say that they cannot predict when he might regain consciousness. He lost a lot of blood and the knife nicked his heart ..." Her breath caught and she had to swallow her pain before continuing. "The doctors told me the surgery went perfectly and he should suffer no long-term ill effects, but also that his age dictates that recovery to full health will take some time and he will need a lot of help."

"Does he live by himself?" Albert asked.

"No, he moved in with me and my husband last year. I don't think he wanted to. Not really, but it was the right time to do it, and I want to spend time with my dad while it's still him."

Albert could think of nothing to say. Alzheimer's seemed to be one of nature's cruellest tricks and he prayed he would find his end long before his own mind began to wander.

Time ticked by, silence ruling the room save for the gentle electronic hum of the machines beside Erich's bed.

The two dogs had laid themselves down, their front paws out straight, their jaws resting against the cool tile. There was nothing going on and therefore no reason to be awake.

Rex opened one lazy eye to find Endal looking his way. When he twitched an eyebrow in question, the labrador started talking.

"*You really chased the men who attacked my human's sire?*"

Rex lifted his head. "*Sure. My human told me to.*"

That got the lab's attention. "*Did you bite them?*"

Rex made a grumpy face. "*No, they cheated. I went after one when they split up, but he jumped on a moped and I couldn't catch him.*"

"*That is cheating.*"

"*I know, right! I've bitten humans before though.*"

"*You have not,*" Endal didn't believe a word.

"*Honest,*" Rex replied. "*I used to be a police dog.*"

"*Used to be?*"

"*Yeah, I got kicked out.*" Rex hated telling this story because there was no way to do it and make himself look good. "*I was too smart for my handlers.*"

Endal laid her head back down. "*They wouldn't use their noses, right?*"

Impressed, Rex said "*Bang on. The clues were always right there in front of them. I could follow the scent to the criminal's house half the time, but would they let me?*"

With the dogs exchanging stories at floor level, Albert's brain supplied a new question to ask.

"Your father was out by himself yesterday?" He was carefully insinuating that it failed to correlate with her concern over her father's deteriorating mind.

"Only for the trip home. We went out for a long lunch, but I got called into work. He insisted he could catch one tram and get off at the right stop." Once again the timbre in Franka's voice showed how angry and upset she was. She blamed herself, which while counterproductive and pointless, was also a natural thing to do. "He was less than half a kilometre from the house when they robbed him. Why would anyone do that?" she wailed, letting her emotions show for the first time since Albert entered the room. "He's just a harmless old man. How desperate for cash must they have been. The cowards." She spat the last remark with venom.

Nodding along, Albert questioned if he was supposed to give comfort, but concluded it was probably time for him to leave. He wanted to check Erich's condition and ask about the name he blurted before passing out and he had done those things. There was nothing more he could do and no reason to think there was anything to gain by digging deeper into the Kurt Berger mystery. With a gentle tug on his lead to get Rex's attention, Albert began to rise from his chair.

He was thinking of ways to announce his departure when Franka apologised.

"Please forgive my outburst, Albert. I'm a little emotional as you might imagine."

"That's perfectly all right my dear. I'm glad your father is going to recover. You should be sure to get some rest for yourself." He chose not to point out how tired she looked, but guessed she had been in the hospital since the previous evening.

With one hand on the door, he opened it a crack and nodded at Rex to get him moving.

Franka stood up to shake Albert's hand, and that was when things went sideways.

Chapter 8

Rex had enjoyed chatting with Endal the labrador; they exchanged stories about what their lives were like and Rex found he was impressed by all the skills Endal possessed. He was just saying his goodbyes and about to leave when his human opened the door and the smells from outside wafted in.

Like an uppercut.

The dual scents of the two men he chased the previous evening hit his nose like an explosion of colour, his body reacting so fast his paws were moving before he'd had a chance to tell them it was go time.

He lunged for the gap, stuffing his head between door and frame to get out. There was no time to spare on waiting for his human to get it open wide enough or to even warn the old man that he was going.

Albert got the scantest of scant warnings, his peripheral vision delivering the news that Rex was about to rip his right arm off before the lead went taut. Mercifully, Albert wasn't holding the lead tight, but when it yanked from his fingers, it pulled the rest of him all the same. He clonked into the half open door, slamming it shut with his barely controlled body a split second after Rex went through it.

Slumped against the door with his face smooshed against the window while he tried to regain his balance, Albert got to see Rex shoot off through the hospital like a furry missile.

"What just happened?" Franka exclaimed, her voice etched with concern. Even with the door closed she could hear Rex barking in the distance yet Albert was still in the room.

Unsticking his face from the glass, Albert yanked the door open again.

"I don't know, but I'm going to find out."

Some distance ahead of him, Rex caught sight of the two men. He didn't know their names and had no idea why they might have attacked the old man last night, but he also didn't much care. His human gave him an order to give chase the previous evening and so far as he was concerned that command remained extant.

They hurt a human – Rex saw the knife one carried when he gave chase and the air had been thick with their victim's blood – and now it was time for him to stop them. The police would come as they always do and he would be praised for catching two criminals. Heck, he might even get a food-based reward; those were the best.

Jonas and Matthias were in the hospital to scope out how hard it might be to get into Erich Janning's room. They carried blades, a perfect tool for the task, and knew the task would take seconds provided they could get to the target. It was the final element that remained unknown. They doubted he would be guarded, though they could not rule it out, but considered the likelihood of visitors to be high. A distraction might be needed, but that was okay, one of them would set off the fire alarm if it came to it. The ensuing confusion would gift them the opportunity they required.

Dressed in suits instead of their usual work clothes, Matthias carried a large camera he'd bought from a thrift shop. They were acting the role of reporters come to interview another hapless victim of Antwerp's criminal underbelly. That was their cover story anyway and it had worked on the lady at the hospital's main reception desk. She gave them directions and commented on how popular Erich Jannings was proving to be.

That information ought to have tipped them off, but even if it had, they wouldn't have suspected the giant German shepherd would be waiting for them. They hadn't even made it to their victim's room when he burst into sight, the enormous mutt with his nasty looking teeth barrelling down the wide hospital corridor towards them.

Matthias had time to register the expletive leaving his colleague's mouth, but was left standing to face the hell hound alone because Jonas was already doing a creditable impersonation of Usain Bolt in the opposite direction.

Matthias dropped the camera, leaving gravity to snatch it from the air as he twisted around and set off as fast as his legs would carry him.

Neither man was happy to be seen off by a dog, but killing it to defend themselves in such a public setting would attract attention and that was the last thing they could afford. It wasn't as though it was a yippy Pomeranian that could be booted out of the way or shut behind a door. The German shepherd looked fit to kill and probably could.

Rex barked, his threats filling the air. They beat him a day ago, both men finding ways to evade his bite, but that was not going to happen a second time.

Jonas barged through a set of double doors, sending the right most flying into the wall with a loud bang. On the other side he encountered a pregnant woman in the early stages of labour. She was holding her husband's hand in a death grip and rubbing her belly as she pleaded with the tiny form inside to make its way to the exit.

The husband, too scared to tell his wife he'd lost feeling in his hand two minutes ago was shocked to see a man in a suit bursting through the door right in front of him.

Jonas couldn't stop in time, but instinct took over to steer him into the man – the woman looked fit to kill. He collided, careening off as he ran through him and kept going.

The husband was tempted to stay on the floor for at least a few seconds in the hope he could massage some life back into his mangled digits, but his wife's glare propelled him back to a sitting position. He was about to get up when the door slammed open again. A second man in a suit, running as though the devil himself was on his heels, checked over his shoulder as he came through and thus missed the sight of the man in his path.

The pregnant woman, incandescent with rage aimed at men in general, aimed a roundhouse punch at Matthais's head. It missed, though only just, and he looked around just in time to see the obstacle in his path. He leapt, legs going wide as they passed either side of the pregnant lady's husband's head.

He pelted onwards, lungs searing and legs pumping.

The right most double door swung back to its original position just in time to make Rex skid to a stop. He could open it, but wasn't going to run through it headfirst at maximum speed. Jumping up onto his back paws, he used his weight to force the door open and when he had enough space to get through, he thundered after his quarry.

Security in the hospital was going berserk, their radios a constant barrage of relayed messages and shouted questions. Everyone was hearing about the rabid dog on the loose, but it was covering ground so fast no one was entirely sure where it was. Or where it was heading.

Albert could hear the commotion ahead of him, but it was getting further away, not closer, and though he gave pursuit, he knew he wouldn't catch up to Rex until he got stuck somewhere or was caught by security.

Rex had no intention of getting caught by anyone. He was in full 'chase and bite' mode. His favourite game at the police dog academy, he was good at it. The double doors between the wards were, however, defeating his best efforts. In the space between them he could almost close the gap to the closest of the two men, but so far Rex's quarry made it to each set of double doors and replenished his lead before Rex could get within biting distance.

Jonas, younger, lighter, and fitter than his partner had gained ten yards on Matthias since they set off and he had almost a ten-yard lead when Matthias started to run. He was far enough ahead now that he was through one set of double doors before Matthias made it to the previous pair.

His lungs heaving from the effort, Jonas chose to stop. The dog almost caught him yesterday. It had to be the same one; there was no chance it was a different giant German Shepherd from hell. He couldn't explain what was going on, but had no need to. Luck had placed him in a quiet part of the hospital and now that he had stopped to get his breath, he devised a far superior plan than running away.

A glance through the window showed Matthias coming his way. He had panic written all over his face and his cheeks were bright scarlet from the effort of sprinting.

Jonas removed his knife from its sheath inside his jacket. The dog wouldn't even see it coming. Matthias would get to the door first, and once through the dog would follow and then he would stick it.

Poised to deliver the blow, he became acutely aware of the sound of running feet coming from the opposite direction. He'd been ignoring them for the last couple of seconds, thinking they were an echo from Matthias's feet, but sparing a glance over his shoulder, he found a trio of hospital security guards coming his way.

They looked about as puffed out as Matthias, but they carried bed sheets and Jonas correctly guessed they were aiming to round up the dog.

Cursing under his breath; he wanted to kill the stupid dog, Jonas yelled, "He's here!" Moving away from the double doors and quickly pocketing his knife, he added, "He's going to bite someone!"

The guards ran toward him and he ran to them, getting behind them just as Matthias burst through the doors.

The poor man had specks of saliva on his chin and cheeks and his tie was flapping in the breeze over his left shoulder. He looked about ready to have a heart attack.

Jonas yelled, "Quick!" and motioned urgently with his right hand. "Run!"

Matthias felt lightheaded, but seeing the light of salvation just a few steps away, he continued running, almost collapsing into his colleague's arms when he got past the trio of hospital security guards.

Rex slowed to push the stupid door open, and was about to keep running when he saw the guards blocking his path.

He barked at them, *"Are you all stupid? The men you want to catch are there! I'm the one chasing them!"* When they continued to advance three abreast, Rex growled, *"Why are humans so stupid!"* There was no way to get past the three men in uniform unless he found a way to jump ten feet in the air and run along the ceiling. The two men he wanted were behind them, slipping away quietly while stealing glances to make sure he could no longer get to them.

Cursing loudly in terms that might have made the security guards blush if they could understand them, Rex about faced and ran back the way he'd come. He was all the way over on the other side of the hospital from where he started, but would have no trouble retracing his steps. All he had to do was follow his own scent.

Unfortunately, before he could get to the next set of double doors a quad of hospital security guards came through it to block his path from that direction too. He checked behind to confirm there was nowhere to go.

Two of the new guards held chairs. Looking very much like amateur lion tamers, they advanced on the terrifying dog. He was hemmed between them and the guards holding sheets. Short of going into a full biting frenzy, there was no chance he could get past them.

Rex parked his butt on the lino, muttering angry insults about the guards and what he suspected their mothers might get up to in alleyways with rottweilers.

Chapter 9

Albert chased Rex for less than a minute before accepting his dog was gone and could have taken any one of a dozen turns to place him anywhere inside the hospital or even beyond its walls. There was no point trying to catch up to him, so when a brace of security guards raced by, undoubtedly on their way to deal with the 'animal problem', Albert went to a window to see if he could spot his dog leaving.

He didn't see Rex, but when Jonas and Matthias exited right in front of Albert, albeit a floor below and the other side of the thick glass, he was looking right at them. They looked different to the night before; their suits altering their image, but the shorter man's hairstyle was distinctive enough to leave Albert with no doubt he was seeing the same two men. Their hastened steps and a furtive glance over one shoulder confirmed they were leaving in a hurry and Albert knew why.

"Well I'll be," he murmured. During their trip around the British Isles, Albert came to acknowledge that Rex was not like the average pooch, so it should have come as no shock that he caught a whiff of the two men from last night and chose to give chase. Albert held no doubt that was the cause of his dog's determined flight. He hadn't caught them, which was disappointing, but the fact that they were at the hospital and must have been close to Erich's room for Rex to have smelled them told a story Albert didn't like one bit.

Returning to Erich's room, Albert confronted Franka. "The two men who attacked your father last night were here. That's who Rex just chased. What is he involved in?"

Franka's hand rose to her mouth in horror.

"Excuse me," interrupted a voice behind Albert.

He was filling the doorway and had to swivel on the balls of his feet to see who had spoken. He groaned internally when he found the frosty nurse glaring up at him.

"Your dog is not allowed to roam where he pleases." She was accompanied by two more of the hospital security guys, neither of whom looked impressed.

"Yes, I need you to call the police," Albert stated firmly.

"I already have, thank you." Nurse Frosty looked smugly pleased with herself.

Albert was about to thank her when his gears churned and he realised they were having two different conversations.

"You called them about me, didn't you?"

"I most certainly did. We can't have dogs running through the hospital. It's not safe. It's not sanitary ..."

Suspecting she was going to carry on listing things 'it wasn't' Albert got in quick.

"The dog was chasing the men who put this man in your hospital," he jerked a thumb at the unconscious form of Erich. "They came back to finish the job, so thank you for calling the police, they will be most interested to hear this latest development."

Nurse Frosty spat, "Utter nonsense," and turned to the guards. "Over to you then. Get on with it."

She got a frown of disapproval from both men, but neither chose to remark. She stepped back out of the way, leaving Albert facing them.

"Sir, you'll need to come with us now. Your dog has been caught and is on its way to the reception area."

"Did you hear nothing I just said?"

Franka stepped in between the men. "He can come with you when the police clear it. Is that understood? My father is in danger, and you are doing nothing to keep him safe." Her tone left no room for argument. Both firm and confident it would be obeyed, Albert found himself wondering what Franka did for a living.

The guards were thrown by her interruption. The one on the left managed to mutter, "That's not what we have been tasked to do."

His colleague managed to sound a little more confident when he said, "Yeah, we don't know anything about anyone being in any danger."

Mercifully, Nurse Frosty had been called away to deal with a patient and the two guards seemed a little lost without her there to whip them along.

Albert seized the opportunity it presented to hit Franka with a question.

"Did anything happen with your father in the last couple of days that stood out to you as unusual or extraordinary?"

Franka opened her mouth to reply, but stopped before she spoke, a thoughtful expression on her face.

Seeing it, Albert persisted, "Even if it is something that seems trivial, it might be worth mentioning."

"Well, there was one incident."

Incident? To Albert's mind it was an unusual word to employ. Most people would say occurrence or event. Incident carried negative connotations. He stayed quiet so she could speak.

The duo of security guards hovered in the doorway, unsure what they were supposed to now do, but educated enough to stay in close proximity to the Englishman they were supposed to be removing.

Franka had Endal lead her back to the chairs where she sat again and started to talk.

"It happened yesterday morning on our way to lunch. I took dad for a walk around Grote Markt, he likes the ambience. He says it's so busy and noisy it reminds him of his days on the trading floor. We were done there and just heading to lunch when he spotted someone. I remember he said ... do you know what, I think he might have called him Kurt."

The name made Albert jolt. The police claimed there was no such man as Kurt Berger, yet it sounded like Franka met him yesterday. Saying nothing, the silence in the room encouraged Franka to continue.

"I'm afraid I might have that wrong. I was saying something to Endal at the time and wasn't really listening. But whether it was Kurt or Chris or something similar, the man got very upset."

"With your dad?" Albert wanted to check he understood how events played out.

"Yes. Dad was a couple of metres away; he left me to speak to the man and he clearly believed that he knew who he was, but he must have been wrong because he started shouting that his name was Dirk De Graaf."

Albert repeated it, "Dirk De Graaf," and pulled out his phone so he could use the notes section to jot it down. He wasn't sure on the spelling but doubted that mattered.

"That's right. I remember dad argued with him, which is really unusual because dad never argues with anyone. I mean, he used to be a lion in the stockbroker industry. We lived in New York for a few years when I was little. He got a job at a trading firm operating out of the World Trade Centre's north tower. Anyway, he thought this Dirk De Graaf was someone he knew ... I really think he might have been calling him Kurt, and Dirk didn't like it. He got quite angry in fact. He was shouting, calling my father a senile old git and saying he needed to get his eyes checked."

"What happened then?" Albert desperately wanted to ask what Dirk De Graaf looked like and was willing to bet money he would match the description of one the two men who attacked Erich. He couldn't though. Franka might have been standing right before the man in question, but only her dog would have seen him.

"Well, he stormed off. I heard him walk away at speed. It upset my father and I thought he would want to talk about it over lunch, but he didn't. I guess he was embarrassed, and I figured it was an Alzheimer's incident. I had thought nothing more of it until you asked about unusual occurrences. Do you think that could have anything to do with what happened?"

Albert shrugged, making the gesture before his brain caught up. "Impossible to tell," he said, since Franka needed a response she could hear. "However, I believe it will be worth looking into." Albert was talking about the police; it was their responsibility to investigate, so Franka's next words caught him off guard.

"Can you do it, Albert?"

Surprised, and not entirely certain he understood her question, he sought to clarify, "Do what, my dear?"

"Investigate? You are kind of famous for it. I can pay you. Hourly rates and all your expenses."

"That won't be necessary."

"Please, Mr Smith. My father was stabbed in the heart and according to you the two men responsible just came back to finish the job. I want to hire you to figure out who attacked him and why."

Albert's mouth was hanging open a little, his brain reeling from the sudden development. What was he supposed to do at this juncture? In a foreign country where he didn't speak any of the languages employed by those around him, was he the right man for the job?

"I'm sure there are better qualified local detectives who would meet your needs …"

"But I want *you*, Mr Smith," Franka insisted. "You already saved my father's life. I owe you more than I can ever repay, yet I need to ask for more."

Albert wanted to continue arguing. He was anything but a young man, he had no jurisdiction or local knowledge, and he was supposed to be on vacation. However, his chance to raise these points exited stage left when the police arrived.

Chapter 10

"Are you simply choosing not to listen or are you just stupid?" Albert demanded to know. He'd been arguing with Lieutenant Bervoets for ten minutes already and felt like he would be just as well served to slam his head into a nearby wall until it left a dent.

The expression on Bervoets' face was the one most people reserve for talking to children. The particularly dense ones.

"Mr Smith, I have explained this three times now, Herr Jannings was the victim of a brutal mugging, nothing more. The descriptions of the two men you saw last night have been circulated and we are actively investigating. This is a matter for the police, not a gentleman from England who likes to think of himself as some kind of sleuth from a mystery novel."

Albert ground his teeth. "What about Dirk De Graaf? The victim, Erich Jannings had an altercation with him in the street mere hours prior to his attack."

Lieutenant Bervoets shook his head, took a deep breath, and tried to be patient.

"Dirk De Graaf is a well-known local businessman and philanthropist. He gives time and money to a glut of local charities and looks nothing like the two men you described. What is it that you would have me believe, Mr Smith? That a respected businessman sent his thugs to kill a harmless old man because he got confused and thought he was someone else? Who are these thugs in this scenario? De Graaf's henchmen?"

His tone was mocking and it made Albert want to pour a bucket of water over the man's head.

"Regardless of who they are or who they might work for, I am reporting that the same two men, who you claim to be nothing more than opportunistic muggers, returned to finish the victim off. That changes everything."

"Were they here to finish him off? How can you know that? Let's assume for one moment that you correctly identified the two men from last night and they really were in this hospital, what possible reason could there be for them to target Erich Jannings? I am quite thorough, Mr Smith. Thorough enough that I looked into Herr Jannings' to find anything that might make him a target. I spoke to his daughter, Franka Schweiger, and confirmed that her father has nothing in his life or his past that could warrant such interest."

"They came after him last night," Albert repeated a point he'd made too many times already. "I watched them select him, follow him, and attack him. If robbery was their intention they would have taken his things and ran, but the mugging was nothing more than a diversion for the real crime – his murder. You can continue to ignore the truth of it, but when they succeed, I will make sure the world is aware of your incompetence."

Albert saw Bervoets tense. His jaw clenched and his eyes narrowed. He wanted to grab Albert and shake some sense into him, at least that was the impression he gave, but he mastered his emotions, and when he spoke again, it came out as a quiet growl.

"I think it is time you were escorted from the premises, Mr Smith."

They stopped en route to collect Rex. The security team for the hospital had a central hub located behind reception. He was led there by a duo of city cops in uniform, both men in their early thirties, going about their business with no sign of emotion – removing the old man was just another task.

He thought that was going to be it, but while he waited for someone to fetch Rex, Lieutenant Bervoets reappeared. Albert thought he'd seen the last of him, but the detective had something more to say.

"I have spoken with the hospital senior administration and they have no wish to press charges. On this occasion," the detective added, making it very clear any further incidents would not be dismissed so readily. "I'm sure you mean well, Mr Smith, but since this is the second time I have spoken to you in less than twenty-four hours, I feel it is wise to caution you."

A frown creased Albert's brow, his ire rising only to be held in check when Bervoets held out a hand, palm extended, and kept right on talking.

"I know who you are, Mr Smith, and I know what you have done. How much of that fantastic tale was true I can only guess, but you are now in a different country and while I encourage you to enjoy all that Antwerp has to offer, I must stress that I do not expect to find myself having a third conversation with you before you leave." He closed his mouth, his eyes drilling into Albert's to hammer the point home. "Do we understand each other, Mr Smith?"

Albert's jaw began to hurt. It wasn't that the detective was incompetent; he might genuinely be good at his job, but he was being offered lines of enquiry and showed no interest in pursuing them. Worse than that, Bervoets seemed to be ignoring the potential danger to Erich Jannings.

"Will you at least place a guard on Erich Janning's door?"

Detective Bervoets snorted a small laugh. "Still going with the conspiracy theory, are we, Mr Smith? I'll tell you what. If I can find anyone to corroborate your story about the two men from last night coming back to finish off Herr Jannings, I will do what I can to have an officer assigned to protect him."

"That's not even nearly good enough," Albert growled.

Suddenly bored of tolerating the Englishman, Bervoets got to his feet and opened the door. "That's as good as you are going to get, Mr Smith."

Angry, when words he might normally bite down on arose, he let them out instead.

"You know what, Detective Bervoets, I don't often meet complete idiots, but if I had a list you would be top of it."

Bervoets gripped Albert's arm, moving him along with a rough tug he wasn't allowed to give, and rather than let him go, he pulled Albert in close so he could growl in his ear, "Don't; cross my path again, old man. You won't like it if you d o."

"Just give me back my dog." A spike of fear shot through Albert's heart. Had he pushed too far? Would Bervoets now decide to call animal services and have Rex detained just to settle some petty need for revenge?

Thankfully, Albert's worries were unfounded and he was reunited with Rex just a few moments later.

"*Hey!*" Rex wagged his tail with excitement and nuzzled Albert's hands when he knelt to fuss his fur. "*I got caught in a net like a fish!*" Rex laughed at himself. "*These idiots stopped me right when I was going to catch the criminals from last night. Can you believe that? They thought I was the problem!*"

Albert made sure Rex was okay, collected his lead and, unopposed, made his way from the hospital. He got a few looks on his way out and could see the security guards watching him, but ignored them all. He'd told Franka he wasn't the right person to investigate her father's attack and that was probably still the case. But right man or not, he was going to stick his nose where it almost certainly wasn't wanted.

His head was so filled with questions and ideas about how he might begin to track down the person or people responsible, that he wasn't paying attention as he exited the hospital via the automatic doors, and almost missed Franka waiting for him with Endal.

That she was there to intercept him wasn't a foregone conclusion, but the dog started to wag its tail and she was standing in the middle of the path which looked like a tactic intended to make her visible. Just to her right and standing behind her shoulder was a man in a suit. It was cheap, a little rumpled, and didn't fit him all that well, but he was clearly with Franka.

"Franka?" he called, closing the distance between them.

"Albert, is that you?"

Albert touched her arm and gave the man to her right a polite nod of greeting. He was somewhere in his sixties with greying hair. His face was shaved smooth and his haircut was less than a week old. There were small spots of dandruff on his collar and shoulders.

He didn't speak and Albert might have remained curious about his identity had Franka not introduced him.

"Albert, this is Josse. He's my driver. Or rather, he's the firm's driver appointed to me. I'm a lawyer," she revealed.

Josse dipped his head again but said nothing. Albert assumed being employed by lawyers making big money decisions all day made him want to stay quiet. Either he had learned that to ask a question resulted in an hour of drivel he couldn't understand, or they simply ignored him.

Addressing Franka, he asked, "Did your father come around?"

"No, I'm afraid not. Did you clear things up with the police?"

Albert genuinely didn't feel that things with the police were clear at all. Lieutenant Bervoets acted as though his story about the two thugs from the previous night was a fabricated tale. Erich needed to be protected, and the police were not going to help until it was too late.

Endal wagged his tail at Rex. *"Hey, what happened to you? You barked a threat and ran off."*

"Yeah, the killers were back. Well, I'm calling them killers, but I guess they actually failed to murder the man they stabbed. Either way, they were in the hospital, so I chased them."

"Did you get to bite one this time?" Endal was unable to hide her excitement at the prospect.

"Nah, the stupid humans got in my way and let them escape."

While the dogs discussed chasing humans at street level, above them Albert was taking Franka's case.

"I don't need any money."

"But I insist," Franka shot back instantly.

"And I insist double," Albert argued, moving on quickly so they could put the matter behind them. "The money would be better served spent on hiring private security to guard your father."

Franka's face expressed her horror. "You really think he's in danger still?"

"It was the same men, Franka. I saw them and Rex must have known who it was because he gave chase the moment he caught their scents." Albert could conceive no other reason why his dog would have taken off the way he did. "If they came twice, they *will* come again, but they won't expect a trained bodyguard positioned outside his door. That's all it will take. Can you handle that?"

He didn't ask if she could afford it, he'd spotted affluence when he first saw her and now he knew she was a lawyer, no doubt remained.

Thinking fast, Franka said, "The firm has used private security in the past a few times. I will make a call."

"Do that now, Franka. Get the ball rolling." Albert saw her reach into her handbag and begin to root around.

"You are going to help me though, aren't you, Albert?" There was an imploring edge to Franka's voice.

"Yes, Franka. I will do what I can to help you identify who was behind your father's attack. I might need some help though. Are you up to that?"

"Of course."

"Right," Albert scratched at an itch on his chin. "Here's what I want you to do."

Chapter 11

Dirk watched the ball fly clean, the resounding thwack from the three wood enough to inform anyone within earshot that it was a good drive. Unfortunately, he wasn't the one holding the club.

It irked him greatly to lose at anything, but already knew his skills on the golf course were not enough to grant him a victory. Not against the mayor.

"Beauty," commented Gene Peeters, the current chief of police who was kissing the mayor's butt because he was looking to retire soon and hoped to move in as his running mate in next year's election campaign. He was right though, the shot was a beauty.

The ball dipped, gravity sucking it back down to earth where it landed some two hundred and fifty metres away. It rolled a farther twenty metres to end up smack in the middle of the fairway. An easy second shot would land it on the green, probably right next to the pin.

Dirk's own drive was on the fairway but only just. It came to rest a few centimetres shy of the rough and on the right side where he would have to bend his second shot around some trees to get it anywhere near the green.

Such was life. Being in the mayor's inner circle or, as Dirk preferred to think of it, letting the mayor be part of his, ticked several boxes on the socially acceptable scale and for that he was prepared to lose a round of golf.

They set off down the fairway, the mayor and the chief of police chatting amiably about nothing much. Their current topic was zonal disputes in the city centre and tariffs applied to exhaust emissions to levy additional taxes from heavy goods vehicles. It was an easy way to make money from businesses that had to enter the area, but Dirk found the subject boring.

He was waiting for them to get to the point of their invite. They enticed him out for a game and thus far had studiously ignored the reason for doing so, acting as though they merely wanted his company.

Dirk didn't believe that for a moment.

It took them until the sixth green, when he had successfully sunk his ball for a par, for them to finally raise the topic of investments.

They wanted his help to increase their investment portfolios and they managed to make it sound as though they were doing him a favour by offering up their paltry savings. It was laughable, but he would do it anyway. He had deals coming up where he would generate a fat profit. It would endear him to the mayor and to the man who might become his deputy.

Dirk thought the chief of police's move into politics was a sure thing, but whether he went that way or not, it would be good to have a voice on his side in the upper echelons of local law enforcement. There would be ways he could retain a chunk of their investments too, rolling it to make even more while assuring them to take it now would half or even quarter their return. It would make them his and that was even better than having them owe him.

Oh, yes, Dirk De Graaf was one of life's winners all right. Playing by the rules was for idiots.

The mayor clapped him on the shoulder and congratulated his putting. He was already six shots ahead and could afford to be complimentary. Dirk wanted to hit him with the club.

Chapter 12

From his 'little chat' with Detective Bervoets, Albert knew Dirk De Graaf was a businessman in the city. It made finding him easy – a task he proudly completed with his phone as a demonstration of recently learned skills. His daughter had insisted he take a phone when he set off on his trip around Britain, and he complied but learned only to use the most basic functions. Over time, he came to accept it might be useful to know a little more, help coming in the form of his youngest grandchild, Apple-Blossom.

From Franka's description of events, her father thought he knew Dirk De Graaf, but had him confused with someone called Kurt Berger. She had been ready to dismiss it as the cognitive fog that comes in the early stages of Alzheimer's, but Albert wasn't so sure. A confused old man would be treated kindly by more than ninety percent of the people he might encounter, at least that was how Albert saw things. Yet if Franka's report was taken at face value, the man Erich thought he knew responded in a manner that Albert regarded as suspicious.

For that reason alone, and not at all because he had not one other lead to follow, he located the building in which Dirk De Graaf worked and aimed himself at it.

Online he found pictures and a bio that listed his qualifications and his role as the CEO of Midas Enterprises.

"Cute name," Albert remarked to himself when he saw it. "Everything he touches turns to gold, does it?" It was a clever marketing ploy for a stockbroker promising to help make rich people richer.

Arriving via tram, Albert found himself at the corner of Grote Markt, the central square in Antwerp. The location was marked loosely on Albert's mental list of places to visit while he was in the city, but he didn't really consider himself to be a tourist. He went looking for food; that was the purpose of taking a trip these days. Staring at buildings and marvelling at the architecture or history bored him and he wasn't afraid to admit it.

It took a few minutes to navigate the huge square to find the building he wanted where, once again, he nodded sagely at the name displayed in huge letters up the side of the front façade: Enterprise House, a name chosen to reflect what went on inside.

Not that it was a house. The building had to be ten stories tall – hardly a sky-scraper, but against the bulk of buildings in the city, it was tall.

The entrance had a rotating door and a fancy reception desk inside made from chrome and glass lit at the front with LEDs. The lobby was three stories tall, the huge space designed to intimidate or impress depending on one's frame of mind.

Beyond the reception desk set to the right and mounted facing into the lobby, not at the entrance doors, lay a security barrier. People going through it were swiping passes. Most wore them around their necks, but others had them attached to short chains on their belts where they could tuck the pass into a back pocket.

A duo of bored looking guards monitored people going in and out, but they were chatting more than they were doing their jobs and only looked animated when one young chap in a group of four couldn't find his pass to swipe the barrier open.

He was directed to the reception desk where Albert saw him receive a new pass just a few moments later. Noting how easy it had been and that the man hadn't been grilled on the location of his pass, Albert devised a plan.

His presence in the lobby had gone unnoticed so far; there were just too many people going here and there and settling in clumps at small tables around the periphery where they held impromptu meetings before moving off again. With a click of his tongue to get Rex moving, Albert went back to the revolving doors.

There he timed his exit to squeeze in at the back of a gaggle of office staff on their way to lunch. One was putting on his jacket still, a garment far too thin and short to ward off the December temperature outside, but which also played right into Albert's hands.

Like many of his colleagues, the man's pass was tucked into his back pocket. The revolving door swept ever onwards, the section with the gaggle of office workers about to close when Albert nipped into it, encouraging Rex to move quickly and making sure to stumble when he slipped inside.

Colliding with the man in the too-thin jacket, Albert apologised and righted himself. Like decent people, the gaggle of male and female staff, all in their late twenties of thirties, checked he was okay and were still doing so when the revolving door spat them into the cold air outside.

He thanked them for their concerns and waved them off feeling just a little guilty about the pass he now held. Hoping it would not cause the young man he'd taken it from any grief, Albert waited until they were out of sight and went back into the building.

His heart rate sped up, a little adrenaline making him feel jumpy, but he crossed the lobby with strides that looked confident even if he didn't feel it. The guards were still chatting, their eyes straying to watch a duo of attractive young women make their way to the elevators at the far end.

Aiming for the middle of five security barriers designed to let one person through at a time -picking the slot next to the guards was asking for trouble and picking the one furthest away would make him look guilty if the pass failed to work - Albert copied what he watched dozens of others do and held his breath.

The barrier, a thick glass thing, slid back into its housing to leave him free to proceed, but as he stepped through a voice called out.

"Wait there please."

Albert felt his jaw clench and he turned to find one of the guards heading his way. Were they paying more attention than he thought? Did the pass flash up a name and image of the person who owned it on a screen somewhere he hadn't spotted? Or was it just obvious he didn't belong?

"You'll need to register the dog, Sir." Upon seeing the relief in Albert's face the guard misread it. He had assumed the old man to be the owner or perhaps a major shareholder of one of the firms in the building and worried he was about to get chewed out for stopping him. Policies were policies though and he was employed to enforce them by the very people who owned and were major shareholders of the businesses in the building. "Sorry, Sir. It's right this way."

Expecting to be caught any second, Albert tried to be surreptitious when he checked the pass to learn the name he expected to have to give. Registering animals coming into the building was a new thing the guard explained in an apologetic tone, coming into force when a woman lost her assistance dog for three hours and it pooped in the boardroom of a billion Euro venture capitalist firm.

"Your name, Sir?"

"Um," Oh, dear Lord, had he forgotten it already?

The guard looked at him expectantly.

"Um, yes, it's Jean Claude ..." he strained his mind to deliver the last name. "Verboom!" he blurted with a gush of relief.

Rex looked up at his human. He could smell the anxiety in the old man's perspiration, but could not identify the cause. He had no idea where they were or why they were here, but that didn't concern him. They were out and being active, which was a lot more fun than sitting around at home.

The guard said, "That's all done, Sir," and used his right arm to indicate that Albert should go freely about his business. When he turned to leave, the guard added, "Thank you," and got a dip of Albert's head in response.

Heart rate slowing, he walked to the bank of elevators. To the right, a shiny glass directory showed the names of the businesses in alphabetical order. Midas Enterprises occupied the top floor and was the only firm up there. It told Albert that Dirk De Graaf was a very successful man which likely dictated that he wouldn't want to speak to an old man asking questions that had nothing to do with making money.

Nevertheless, Albert was determined to look him in the eye and learn if there was anything more to the incident with Erich than an unfortunate case of mistaken identity.

Chapter 13

The elevator took Albert and Rex all the way to the top floor where it opened into a plush lobby. Frosted glass panelling opposite the doors displayed the name of the firm.

Rex sniffed the air, sucking in a deep noseful to see what it contained. The answer was very little. He found one scent and it was old. No one had been here for at least a day.

Albert led him to the door, which was locked. That didn't strike him as strange until he looked about for a buzzer or intercom and failed to find one. He looked back at the elevator but there was nothing there either.

Perplexed, he poked the one panel he could see, a scanner much like they had in the building's main entrance lobby. A person wanting to gain access would tap their card against the reader and the door would unlock.

Probably, Albert surmised.

Frowning, he exhaled a slow breath and questioned what he was seeing. No sound came from within, no snatches of conversation, no ringing phone, and nothing to indicate there was anyone on the other side of the frosted glass.

Finding a small gap where the door met the frame, Albert pressed his face against it and squinted. By moving his head to the left and right he could create what was possibly a 30° angle. He could see desks and chairs and computers - workstations set up and ready to be used. However, he'd expected the floor to be filled with brokers doing deals on their phones or hunched over their computers analysing ... well, whatever it was stockbrokers analysed.

Albert knew nothing about the financial world beyond the simple fact that he'd never earned enough money to get into trouble.

The expected stockbrokers were absent though and the floor of the open plan business was eerily quiet. Unsure what to make of it, Albert was turning to leave when another elevator arrived with a ping.

The doors slid open to reveal three men. Two wore casual suits and had curly wires leading from under their shirt collars to their left ears. Albert judged them both to be in their thirties. They had what he would refer to as an ex-military vibe which is to say that they looked competent, capable, and not the sort of person one ought to mess with.

Their features were middle eastern; Turkish or Syrian Albert guessed. They wore their black hair short on their heads and faces, both sporting trim beards. Facially, they were similar enough to give away their shared parentage. They observed Albert and his dog, their eyes swiftly assessing the level of threat in what appeared to be a practiced move.

The third man wore chinos with a polo shirt, and sweater. He had a sports jacket draped over his left arm. Albert noted the shallow impressions in the skin of his left hand where a glove had recently been. His right hand had no such indentations. That and his choice of outfit denoted that he'd been playing golf.

He had greying hair with only a few sprinkles of the original dark brown showing through. At six feet tall and roughly sixty years old, Albert believed he would have been considered tall in his younger years. He was carrying a slight bulge to his belly where middle age had claimed his waistline, but overall he had an athletic frame, like that of a sports star who had been in good shape for most of his life, but was letting it go now that the years were creeping on. His face had good symmetry with a strong jaw and intelligent eyes.

Albert recognised him from pictures he'd found using his phone less than an hour ago.

"Dirk De Graaf. Pleased to meet you. My name is Albert Smith." The men were out of the elevator and heading his way, so Albert extended his hand, expecting Dirk De Graaf to take it.

Instead, the owner of Midas Enterprises chose to stare right at him, his jaw moving left to right as though he were trying to decide what response he wanted to give.

His right arm still hanging in the air, Albert allowed it to drop back to his side; clearly it was not going to be shaken anytime soon.

Rex sniffed at the three men, sampling their odours to see if he could discern why his human had brought him here. They were embroiled in a mystery surrounding a crime once again and he assumed it was something to do with that. Rex enjoyed using his nose to solve crimes, especially since his human had learned to pay attention, but his skillset could not always place him where he needed to be. That was where Albert came in and he liked how they complemented each other.

The three men, however, did not smell of anything familiar, and certainly bore no trace of the two criminals he chased through the hospital.

"What is it that you think I can do for you, Mr. Smith?"

Several seconds had passed between Albert introducing himself and Dirk De Graaf opening his mouth to speak for the first time. He was rude, but the rich often were in Albert's experience.

Getting straight to the point, Albert said, "You met a man yesterday. His name is Erich Jannings. Do you know him?" Albert watched Dirk's face to see what emotions might pass over it. If he had something to hide, or was about to lie, Albert believed that he would see it.

Defeating him, Dirk looked down, sighed, and then looked back up. "Are you referring to the poor, confused old man who accosted me in the street yesterday?"

"Was he confused?" Albert challenged.

The question brought a smile and a chuckle. "Well he kept calling me by somebody else's name. I should say he was rather confused, wouldn't you?"

He was dancing with a skilled opponent, that much was obvious from the opening salvos. Dirk De Graaf gave nothing away and his security had positioned themselves either side of Albert to bookend him. They were doing nothing to suggest they might act without the say so of their boss, but they were trying to look intimidating.

Changing his approach, Albert said, "He was attacked last night."

Dirk gasped, showing his surprise and horror. "Attacked? By who? I'm sure you don't think I had anything to do with it."

"Your encounter with him became quite heated, Mr De Graaf. Why was that?" He deliberately brushed over the question of Dirk's involvement in the attack, leaving it so he could circle back if necessary but already wondering if the rich stockbroker could somehow be behind it.

Dirk blinked and tilted his head, a questioning frown creating ridges on his forehead.

"I'm sorry, I'm not sure I understand what your role is here, Mr Smith. You're clearly not the police and I'm not sure why it is that you think I should be answering your questions."

Albert's eyes narrowed automatically, and he had to force the warmth into the smile he gave.

"I'm just asking a few questions, Mr De Graaf. A man was brutally assaulted and almost died from a knife wound inflicted by one of his assailants. The attack appears to have no motive," Albert omitted the theft of Erich's wallet, phone, and watch, "and the only remarkable thing that has happened to him recently is his encounter with you. So, I ask again, why did you become so angry with him?"

Dirk eyed the old man silently. When the elevator doors opened and he first saw him, the recognition was immediate, but he could not work out where he knew him from. It continued to bother him until a few seconds ago when his brain finally figured it out. He gave his name as Albert Smith and now Dirk could visualise the headlines and photographs that appeared in the newspapers and the TV several months ago. He'd paid little attention to the story; he was too busy to care, but recalled how the media channels romanticised it. They made the old man out to be a hero; the saviour of a community held captive underground at the whim of a madman.

Now he was here and poking around in affairs that were going to get him killed. He'd already sent Jonas and Matthias to kill him, though of course, he was just a nameless old man with a dog at that point. Now he knew who he was dealing with nothing changed.

"I believe, Mr Smith, that you have overstayed your welcome. My associates will show you from the building."

The henchmen moved in from either side, coming for Albert until Rex gave them a warning growl that caused them both to pause.

Albert was going to leave; there was nothing to gain by letting Rex bare his teeth to defend them both, but he had one final question and made sure to hold Dirk's gaze when he delivered it.

"Who is Kurt Berger?"

The skin around Dirk's eyes tightened rapidly and he nodded his head at the men either side of Albert. Moving swiftly, the man to Albert's left – the one farthest from Rex, produced a stun gun from inside his jacket.

Rex had no clue what was happening, but could smell the tension in the room and had been ready to defend his human almost since the three men left the elevator. Seeing a weapon appear, Rex lunged and it was then that the other man jabbed a stun gun into the fur on his right flank.

Rex felt his muscles spasm and knew nothing more.

"Works on dogs then," the man to Albert's right remarked, his face matching the chipper, upbeat tone of his voice.

Startled by the unexpected turn of events, Albert didn't even get time to register what happened to Rex before a spark flashed under his left ear and everything went dark.

Chapter 14

Albert came to in the elevator, groggily raising his head as he tried to make sense of his environment. He was dangling between the two men, each of them with a hand hooked under an arm to suspend him off the floor.

Blinking dreamily, he found Rex lying against the right hand wall. His dog was still unconscious, but he could see Rex's chest rising and falling.

"It would be simpler to do it now," Medhi remarked.

"Boss says it's too risky," replied his brother, Billal. "There're too many cameras in the building. Even the parking garage has them."

Coupled to those inconvenient facts was the alert building security had sent out. Jean Claude Verboom had returned from his quick run to the local café with his coworkers to discover his pass was missing. That the system had recorded him swiping in ten minutes earlier caused a check of the security cameras and in turn a building wide alert with Albert's face and description.

Dirk De Graaf wasn't happy about it – he wanted to dispose of the old man and his dog with immediate effect – however, the likelihood someone would track his movements and know he had visited the top floor was too great. Admitting he had the troublemaker was the only sensible option. He alerted security so they would be waiting in the lobby and reported the old man had been threatening.

"We'll pick him up again later."

"Him and the dog," Billal agreed.

The car slowed, a ping announcing their arrival and the doors opened to reveal the building's gargantuan lobby. There were less people about than earlier – Albert arrived during the lunch rush and most of the workers were either out to lunch now or back at their desks.

It took some concentration to lift his head, but the sensation was returning to his limbs and he found he could clench his fists and wiggle his toes.

"Right, you get the dog. I'll take grandpa here."

"I can walk," Albert mumbled just when the man now holding both his arms began to drag him from the elevator.

The henchman paid him no attention, flipping him over so he could walk backward with Albert's legs trailing. He tried to get them under his body but lacked the coordination to pull it off. The other man grabbed Rex by one back leg and followed, Rex looking like nothing more than a sack of stuffed fur.

It made Albert angry and he began to fight back.

"Let go of me!" he shouted loudly. There were already a bunch of people in suits and office wear watching the spectacle, and more heads turned to see now as he continued to demand the man let him go.

"Okay, Jean Claude Verboom. Whatever you say," the man replied, making no attempt to do anything of the sort. They were almost at the security barriers where a new commotion could be heard.

"Okay, put him down," commanded a new voice that wasn't a new voice at all, Albert realised with a groan.

This time the henchman holding his arms complied and Albert had to fight not to crack the back of his skull off the tiles when he was abruptly released.

Incensed and wishing he still had the strength of his youth to crack Dirk's henchmen a good 'un on their smug faces, he got his hands and feet arranged so he could get up and stood to find Lieutenant Bervoets observing him with a single raised eyebrow.

Speaking through gritted teeth, Albert said, "I'm going to check my dog." Clearly Bervoets didn't see Albert as a threat because he made no attempt to stop him when he turned and on wobbly legs crouched to make sure Rex was okay.

Rex was just coming around. His mouth was dry and his nose itched. He also had a strange craving for pizza. His legs felt disconnected from the rest of his body and when he tried to get up he succeeded only in rolling over onto his other side.

"What happened?" he asked Albert. *"I was supposed to be biting someone,"* Rex stopped to lick the itch on his nose and missed, going cross-eyed in the process, *" but now I'm here."*

Alberts limbs were behaving more or less as they should, so he lowered himself to the floor and cradled Rex in his arms. A pair of uniformed cops loomed over them, doing nothing, but clearly waiting for instruction. One had his hands on his cuffs where they sat on his belt and Albert could see what was going to happen next.

Lieutenant Bervoets had moved to one side where he was speaking quietly with Dirk De Graaf's 'associates'. He saw when they handed over a security pass, undoubtedly the one Albert swiped to gain entry. He took notes and placed the pass in a small, clear evidence bag.

Albert was angry with himself, but not for the steps he took or for getting caught; there was always a risk he wouldn't make it back outside without being discovered. No, he was angry in principle. Angry at the world in general. His imminent arrest and incarceration were unjust and there was nothing he could do about it.

Dirk De Graaf was behind the attempted murder of Erich Jannings; of that he was now certain. He had not the slightest idea why, but figuring such things out was at the same time the most frustrating and most rewarding part of any investigation and he relished the sense of victory that would come from seeing the tables turned.

Rex stretched his legs. The sensation had returned, and he felt confident he could get up if he wanted to. Cradled in his human's arms though, he was content to stay where he was. He could see the police – all cops wear a derivation of the same uniform – and figured that meant nothing bad was going to happen to his human for the time being. That was good because he didn't exactly feel up to the task of defending him.

Albert watched for Bervoets' return, but made no attempt to get up when he did. De Graaf's men went to the elevator, only looking in his direction when they were inside and waiting for the doors to close. Their faces were expressionless, unreadable, but one winked in the moment before the doors stole him from view.

"Mr Smith, you are having quite a day."

"They attacked me with a stun gun," Albert spat in reply. He knew it was futile to argue, but did it anyway. Anything less was the same as admitting he was wrong.

"They claim that you confronted their employer, Dirk De Graaf, and became violent. They stunned you because it was the safest way to prevent anyone from being hurt."

"I'm nearly eighty, man! What was I going to do against those two?"

"Apparently, you set your dog on them, just like you sent him racing through the hospital earlier today. Is your dog dangerous, Mr Smith?"

"No, he is not, and I didn't set him on anyone. I already told you why he ran through the hospital."

"Ah, yes. He was chasing the bad men who attacked Erich Jannings."

"*That's right*," Rex wagged his tail.

Detective Bervoets dropped into a crouch, so his head and eyes were almost level with Albert's.

"You stole a security pass, broke into a building, and threatened a respected member of the community. You were a police officer, were you not, Mr Smith? Do I really need to explain what is going to happen next? Can I expect your cooperation?"

Albert could have shouted and ranted, or argued that Bervoets was both blind and stupid, but he didn't. Aiming plea-filled eyes at the detective, he asked, "Will you make sure Rex is taken care of?"

Chapter 15

Rex watched his human being led away. Albert was with two police officers and in handcuffs, which confused him. He was being held on his lead by a third officer and following Albert to the doors that led back outside.

This was a good thing because he really needed to pee. He might have fought against the new person, a woman, holding his lead but his human told him not to. Human behaviour defied explanation most of the time anyway, but today the people around him were bewildering.

That his human had been arrested was the part he understood the least. It made no sense at all. They were the ones who solved the crimes and caught the bad people, and the police were supposed to help them, not get in their way.

However, when they exited the building, there was an animal services van waiting outside and Rex could smell stale fear radiating off the vehicle's insides. He bucked, trying to pull away from the police officer holding him. Seeing him start to fight, the animal services guys sprang into action, but they had expected an easy handover of a placid dog and their control poles were still in the rack in the back of the van.

Albert was at the police car and about to be loaded inside when he saw the commotion behind him.

He shouted, "Rex no!" but it was too late to prevent the panic driving his dog's frenzied escape attempt.

The police officer held on with all her strength and was winning, but Rex had tricks ready to deploy.

Changing direction, he ran through the woman's legs and might have flipped her had she not reacted so fast. Surprised to find his tactic fail, Rex opted for the strategy of last resort. He turned to face her, ducked his head and pushed away. The collar caught on his ears and jaw, crushing his larynx until it popped free.

The animal services chaps ran to intercept, their control poles at the ready, but they were too late, and Rex was gone. He'd been taken by the dog catchers before and wasn't lining up to let it happen again.

Tail between his legs, Rex ran, fleeing across the busy Grote Markt square to get away.

Behind him, Albert was pushed, gently but forcibly into the back of the police car. He was trying to see where Rex went and praying the animal services guys would catch him. Antwerp was too big of a city for a dog to wander and be found again. Would he stay in the general area?

It wasn't the first time Rex had run off, and due to that fact they had visited his local vet back in England where Rex received a tracking chip in his shoulder. It connected to an App on his phone and could be traced by the firm making them as well. It might not make Rex easy to find, but at least he would find him.

Rex didn't know any of this and wasn't thinking about Albert. His thoughts were attuned to being somewhere the animal services guys with their catchpoles were not. He'd been taken into custody before and was anything but a fan. They would look after him, sort of, which is to say they would make sure he had food and water and would have a vet carry out a thorough examination to ensure he was in good health.

However, the food was a brand so budget Rex would rather eat a dead badger coated in kitty litter from a well-used tray, and the thorough examination always required someone to stick something up an orifice he thought of as an out valve only.

He was better off running and he knew it.

Only once he was on the other side of the square and confident he had given the humans the slip did he stop to figure out where he was. This allowed him to focus on what he could smell and in turn that meant he became aware of all the food.

The air reeked of it. Spices and herbs, sugar and salt, meat, sweet, and savoury. Rex didn't need anything to eat but he was instantly hungry. Looking around there were stalls in every direction, the market bustling with activity. It dominated one half of the square and he'd missed most of it by running around the outside.

The only issue Rex could perceive with his current need to eat everything in sight was the worrying fact that his human was not with him. The old man's absence and where he might now be was a concern he would need to deal with. The bigger issue at that precise moment was how he would get some food without Albert there to supply it.

He had a rudimentary concept about money. Humans had bits of paper they would fight and even kill for which they exchanged for things they wanted. It was mystifying to Rex and all canine kind, yet what he understood was that he couldn't get the humans at the stalls to give him anything to eat without it.

That wasn't going to stop him though. Stealing food fell right into the 'bad dog' category, but without Albert around to assist it became his only option.

But what to have?

The solution presented itself sooner than expected when a child dropped the slice of pizza he was holding. It hit the floor twenty yards to Rex's front, his eyes going wide and his paws starting to move until the child bent down and picked it up again.

Deflated, Rex's excitement returned a heartbeat later when the child's mother knocked it from his hand. Admonishing him, she dragged him back to the stall to get another piece and Rex swooped.

He swooped fast too because he was not the only one who saw it hit the ground.

Chapter 16

There were other dogs in the marketplace, their eyes and noses attuned to spot any food that might be dropped. They hid under tables and in the shadows between the stalls, but Rex could both see and smell them.

He moved fast, grabbing the slice of pizza without pausing to slow down. He expected to be chased – the other dogs looked hungry and they smelled like strays which made their behaviour unpredictable. There were strays in every city and town, Rex knew that. Heck, he'd met some last night. In general he gave them a wide berth, but he couldn't help his curious glance to check out if the sexy springer spaniel was around.

Too busy looking for her, he almost collided with a pushchair and had to swerve fast to miss it. Doing so took him under a stall where he encountered the same Jack Russell cross from the previous evening.

He snapped his teeth at the pizza hanging from Rex's mouth and almost got a bite. Rex changed direction again, angling to get away from the strays who were everywhere under and around the market stalls.

Seeing daylight and empty space through a gap in the canvas, Rex ran from the market, his prize gripped between his teeth, and into the open part of the square to send pigeons scattering in every direction. Stealing a look over his shoulder, he noted with some surprise that none of the strays were following. They had given up already.

Telling himself they were wise enough to realise he was a well-fed, large dog in his prime and not to be messed with, Rex dropped the pizza and puffed out his chest.

It was at that precise moment that a slither of worry crept up his spine.

The strays were watching him. Lining the back apron of the rearmost stalls where they all faced inward, the dogs' faces displayed no disappointment at missing out on the pizza. In fact, they reminded him of spectators getting ready to watch something interesting.

A pigeon landed right in front of his nose. It cooed curiously, tilting its head sideways to view Rex from a different angle.

"*Shoo, birdy*," he growled.

A second pigeon landed, this one twice the size and weight of the first. Then a third and fourth. The strays were jostling to get a better position, the smaller dogs trying to climb on someone else's back to improve their view.

Frowning, Rex lowered his head to reclaim the pizza and that was when the flock hit him.

One moment he was looking at four pigeons, the next all he could see was feathers, weird, clawed feet, beaks, and beady eyes. Hundreds of them descended on him, divebombing to distract and confuddle his senses while yet more of them devoured the pizza.

The slice, covered in feathers, grime, and grit was borne aloft in several pieces. The attack flock dispersed at that point, abandoning Rex to pursue the food they came for.

Rex staggered to his left, tried to right himself and staggered to his right when he overcompensated. His eyes felt like they were revolving individually and out of sync with each other.

"*Come on!*" he tried weakly. "*I'll have you all!*"

Still trying to clear his utterly discombobulated brain, Rex had to focus hard to stop the world spinning when he heard sniggering.

The strays had ventured out from their hiding places, more than a dozen of them approaching across the empty square.

"*Don't you know nothing?*" laughed a mostly bulldog mix. "*Never go out into the open. The pigeons will always get you.*"

"*Aww, give him a break, Rufus. Can't you see he's new to this?*"

Just as it had the first time he heard it, the springer spaniel's voice zipped through Rex's body on a straight line path to his groin.

The pizza was long gone, pecked into pieces and scattered between the flock of pigeons who departed almost as fast as they attacked. Shaking his head to clear it, Rex turned to face her while fixing a confident smile on his face. Puffing out his chest to make his body look bigger overall, the whole show might have worked if he didn't have a dozen feathers sticking out of his teeth, ears, and eyebrows.

The spaniel sniggered. *"You're such a doofus. What's your name?"*

Confidence waning, Rex glanced at the pack of strays now surrounding him. They were all amused by him; a sentiment he wasn't used to. He was big and impressive, he knew that, and was used to having other dogs look at him with a degree of awe.

"Um, Rex?" he managed to mumble, still trying to convince his head to stop spinning. He felt like lying down. He felt like throwing up, but he couldn't do either of those things with the sultry spaniel watching. Instead, he toughed it out, doing his best to pretend the pigeons hadn't bothered him at all.

"Well, Um Rex," the spaniel winked mischievously, *"You look like you could do with a friend."*

The observation came loaded with suggestion which made Rex question where he stood. She called him a doofus then winked at him. Talk about mixed signals.

"What happened?" she asked. *"Human abandoned you?"* She sniffed at the air around him. *"I can still smell domestication on you. Yesterday you said you still had a human, but you don't, do you? You've been abandoned and you just don't want to admit it."*

A bloodhound, one he'd seen last night, sidled up next to him, nudging one shoulder against Rex's in a comradely manner.

"It's okay, brother. It happened to all of us. Come join our family. We could use a big fella like you. We can teach you the right way to survive on the street, so you won't end up being pecked to death by the pigeons a second time." The last remark was delivered with the bloodhound failing to keep a straight face and the rest of the strays laughing along. They had enjoyed watching the pigeons get the better of him.

"I still have a human," Rex replied reflexively and a little too fast. *"And I'll be ready for the pigeons next time."*

"Oh, sweetie," the spaniel laughed, *"only crazy dogs with a screw loose challenge the air rats. There are too many of them and they are organised."*

"We can be organised too," Rex argued.

"We?" questioned the Jack Russell cross. *"What's this 'we'? You still have a human. At least that's what we all just heard you say. You're not one of us."*

"Maybe not, but that doesn't change anything. If you want the pigeons' respect you have to take it."

His suggestion drew chuckles from the assembled strays.

"I'm Shania," the spaniel finally introduced herself. *"This is Plug,"* she nodded to the Pitbull who grinned so wide his face took on the appearance of a surprised coconut. *"The bichon is Fleabag."* At the sound of his name, Fleabag looked around, one back leg hanging guiltily in the air where it had just been feverishly scratching at his neck. *"Then we have Jack, and Russell,"* a second Jack Russell cross popped up next to the first. Shania went on to introduce the rest of her pack. Quite how she had risen to be the alpha Rex could only wonder, but she ruled over dogs far bigger and meaner than her and none of them saw any reason to question it.

She proved this a moment later, when she dismissed them all. *"Go about your business now. I have something to discuss with Rex."*

They were starting to drift away, heading back to the market where they vanished under the stalls once more.

Shania jinked her head for him to follow, the suggestive smile back in place when she set off toward the far end of the market away from her pack.

Loping along behind like an obedient puppy, his mind conjuring images of what he thought (hoped) was to come, Rex had forgotten his human and that he'd last seen the old man getting taken away by the police.

"Where are we going?" Rex asked.

Shania didn't respond, she just shot a cheeky glance over one shoulder. However, when they reached the far corner of the market, she nipped through a gap between stalls and was waiting for Rex on the other side.

"Hey, Big Boy," she batted her eyelids when he stuck his head through the gap to see where she had gone. *"I need a mate and I'm not picking from the mongrels in my pack. Can I assume you are unattached? No lady and pups waiting for you at home?"*

"No, I am very much unattached," Rex had to check that he wasn't dribbling. It was very much 'Go Time' and it had been too long since he'd had the chance to experience this side of life.

Shania was looking right into his eyes, the brash confidence he'd seen until now no longer present, replaced by a vulnerability that made him want her even more. His right front paw was just about to start moving when a bark of alarm burst through the moment.

"It's the fuzz! Leg it!"

Plug the Pitbull burst into their private space in the back area behind a market stall, but he didn't stop to deliver an additional message, he ran straight through and out the other side. Rex watched him go and was lining up something cool to say about some dogs being unable to keep their heads when danger came knocking when he spotted an inconvenient fact: Shania was no longer with him.

She had legged it in the other direction, back into the market where she was barking to guide her pack of strays away from the danger.

Unsure which way to go, Rex backed out of the canvas.

The fuzz in question were the animal services guys who had spent the last two minutes sneaking up on Rex from behind. His backend had been sticking out of the canvas, presenting an easy and obvious target. Counting down to three, they pounced.

Back in the open, Rex twisted around to find a tall man coming right for him, control pole extended, the loop for his neck open and ready. Automatically, Rex turned away and started to run ... straight into the second animal control guy coming the other way.

Chapter 17

It was early evening and full dark outside when the police released Albert. He was shocked to be let out, expecting they would keep him in until the morning. He discovered why though when Bervoets appeared while he was being processed.

"Mr De Graaf is not pressing charges and neither are the people at Enterprise house. You should think yourself lucky, Mr Smith. That's the second mess you have caused and gotten away with today."

Albert huffed out a breath of frustration. It was good that he could go, but he could easily explain why De Graaf didn't wish to press charges – he wanted him dead. That was far harder to achieve while he was in police custody. Thankfully, Albert mused. It would have been hard to escape harm if it came for him while incarcerated.

Rex was at the animal services building – he found out when they came to get him from his cell – but inconveniently that wasn't located near the station. A taxi would get him from A to B, but getting Rex back wouldn't fix his problems.

Pocketing his wallet, phone, and loose change, Albert took a moment to strap his watch back on his right wrist before meeting Lieutenant Bervoets' gaze.

"I'm sure it goes without saying that should there be yet another incident you will not be released so swiftly. My advice is to pack your things and leave Antwerp, Mr Smith. It might be better for everyone if you did."

Jolting him, a fresh thought occurred. Was Bervoets in De Graaf's pocket? The man had money and power, two things that had caused many a law enforcement officer to stray in the past. Once they take that first bribe or paycheck, there is no way back. He couldn't tell if he was right, but it remained a concern.

Picking his next words carefully, Albert said, "I will be leaving my accommodation the moment I get back to it. I can assure you of that."

The response pleased Bervoets, the detective's shoulders slumping a touch as though a burden had just been removed.

"Very good, Mr Smith. I think that is the wisest decision."

Albert didn't care what he thought. He wanted to beg that Bervoets investigate Dirk De Graaf if his body found its way to the morgue in the next day or so. They would come for him; he knew that much, so he would make it hard for them to find him. However, his concern that Bervoets might be involved stilled his tongue. He needed to get out of the station, collect Rex, and come up with a plan that would get him to the morning in one piece.

He was being pushed to leave by all parties except one. Franka wanted him to stay and were he to abandon her and leave, her father would surely pay with his life. Albert had uncovered something, or rather Erich Jannings had, and Albert's self-appointed task was to figure out what it could be.

With all his confiscated possessions returned, Albert left without another word. He didn't have time to speak anyway, he had too much to do and an all-powerful need to eat. There had been nothing since breakfast what with one thing and another, but dinner would have to wait. He was collecting Rex first.

Leaving the station via a door at the back, he was escorted around the side by a junior officer who used his radio to have a gate opened. Once through it, Albert was on his own and suddenly questioned if De Graaf's henchmen might be waiting for him in the shadows nearby.

If he was right about Bervoets, and he figured it was fifty-fifty that the detective was dirty, then he could have called ahead to make sure they were ready. His heart thumping harder than he liked, Albert felt a little naked in the dark without Rex around.

Fear made his lip curl, his ire rising that he had genuine reason to worry for his safety. Well, if they were there he was going to meet them head on, not cowering in the dark. Emboldening his stride, Albert marched into the street. It was lit from above by overhead lights and completely devoid of stun gun wielding henchmen so far as he could see.

There were no taxis nearby, nor a taxi rank at which he could wait. Of course, police stations are not exactly hubs of commerce or tourism that might demand one.

He walked, pulling his coat tight around his body and donning his flat cap to keep as much warmth in as possible. Spotting a taxi coming toward him on the other side of the road, he raised an arm and waved, thanking his lucky stars when it cruised to walking pace and swung around to pick him up.

Nestled in the warmth of its embrace, Albert sunk into the backseat. The cabbie said it was a ten-minute drive to get to the animal services place, an estimate that proved accurate. He left a worthwhile tip and asked where he could find another cab when he had his dog back. The cabbie offered to wait – fares were all too few and far between at this time of the year.

Hoping that might work out and he would find him still outside after however long it took to get Rex back, Albert buzzed the bell and pushed the door when a disembodied voice invited him inside. He was made to wait, but at the twenty-minute point when he was becoming frustrated and annoyed because the taxi was unlikely to still be waiting, a door to his right opened and Rex appeared.

Seeing his human, the German shepherd dragged the handler across the tile to get to him, his tail wagging so fast it made a blur in the air.

"Hey, boy!" Albert got down onto one knee to fuss Rex's fur and let him nuzzle. There was paperwork to sign, but he'd already shown his ID and had the App for the tracking chip in Rex's neck on his phone as proof of ownership.

Two minutes later they were outside once more where Albert breathed a sigh of relief to find the taxi exactly where he left it.

"Where to next?" the cabbie needed a destination, and Albert almost gave the name of his hotel. If De Graaf's men were going to strike, a hotel room in the middle of the night was a great place to do it. They might hedge that he would take Rex out before settling down to sleep and they would be right. What better time to spring an ambush?

He needed to go somewhere else and he couldn't risk going back to get his things in case they were already staking the place out. They would see and they would follow, following through with their plan just the same but at a different location. Hoping they were not so well informed that they were already watching him collect Rex, he asked the cabbie to take him to a hotel in the De Leien suburb. Franka lived there and he knew it to be upmarket and therefore safer than many parts of the city at night.

It would be pricey, but that hardly mattered. Besides, he had neither pyjamas nor the basic sundries such as soap and a toothbrush; a higher end hotel would be able to provide such items even if they came at a price.

Chapter 18

The cabbie took him to Hotel Palais De le Court, where the cost for his room for the night was less than he'd mentally budgeted which came as a pleasant surprise. He wasn't short of money and had little need for it other than to support his daily needs and travel expenses. Nevertheless, a lifetime of having less than he wanted made him prudent with what he had and being frivolous was not in his nature.

However, upon reaching his room he discovered a problem: he had no food for Rex.

Rex was sitting on the carpet looking expectantly at his human. It was past dinner time and his belly had registered empty more than an hour ago.

"Right," Albert clapped his hands together. "I guess we are eating out tonight, old boy. What cuisine do you fancy?"

The tone of Albert's voice would have been enough to get Rex up and excited, but the suggestion of food was firing his tastebuds into overdrive.

"*Oooh, how about some street pizza?*" Rex barked, recalling the treat he didn't get to eat earlier.

Mentally translating his dog's bark for 'Yes,' Albert made sure he had the swipe card for his door, turned off the lights, and headed back down to the lobby with Rex dancing by his side.

At the elevators his phone began to ring and fishing it from his coat pocket he found Franka's name displayed on the screen.

"Albert, I have some information to share," she said by way of greeting. "Do you want to come to me or the other way around?"

An automatic need to give the blind woman the easier option arose instinctively though he quashed it before his lips could betray his Victorian thinking. Franka was a capable, intelligent woman and he doubted there was much she couldn't do for herself. Especially not with Endal at her side.

Regardless, it was probably better that he went to her. She would have a computer and though his knowledge of how to use one to find information was rudimentary, he suspected Franka would yet again be able to help. Also ...

"I don't suppose you could spare a bowl of doggy chow, could you?"

Having explained his predicament, even though he played it down and brushed over his brief incarceration, it came as no surprise when Franka insisted he come for dinner. She then dispatched her husband to collect him from the hotel.

While he waited, and to appease Rex, Albert found the hotel bar where he ordered himself a gin and tonic and fed Rex a packet of crisps. It wasn't much, but it was a whole lot better than nothing. The barman supplied a bowl with some water for Rex to slake his thirst and in the quiet corner of the bar where he stuck himself, Albert pondered the case.

Dirk De Graaf had a secret, of that he was certain. What it was he had no clue, but he was willing to believe Erich Jannings triggered a defence mechanism that resulted in his attempted murder.

Dirk sent two lackies to commit the crime and it was pure luck they didn't succeed. The question troubling him more than any other was to do with why a successful businessman would have any involvement in such shady, criminal dealings. Not businessman, Albert corrected himself, Dirk De Graaf was a stockbroker.

And so was Erich Jannings. Franka had said so.

Why hadn't that occurred to him before? There could be something in it, a connection between them. Past dealings? Something that went bad or perhaps went really well, but wasn't the kind of deal you ever talked about again. Albert couldn't explain how to short a stock, but he knew greedy investors could be found guilty of insider trading. Had Erich stirred up something from the past when he approached Dirk in the street?

Albert took a sip of his drink and asked himself another question: What did any of that have to do with Kurt Berger and just who the heck was he?

He was just finishing his drink when he heard a person asking for Albert Smith. It was a man's voice and echoing through into the bar from the hotel's receptions desk around the corner. With a click of his tongue, Albert got Rex moving.

Waiting near the long counter of the reception desk which was manned by three overly attractive and young members of the hotel staff, a tall, thin man with a coat over his arm was checking his watch.

"Mr Schweiger?" Albert enquired.

He looked up, saw the old man with the German Shepherd, and extended his hand.

"Jean." He had a firm grip. "And you must be the famous Albert Smith."

Albert grimaced. "Just Albert, please. I'm no one special."

Jean released his hand and with his right arm steered Albert toward the exit.

"I think you are being modest, Albert, and my wife would heartily agree. She thinks you are the most wonderful man on the planet. First you save her father's life, scaring away a pair of criminals not once but twice, and then you offer to help figure out why someone wants him dead and top it off by refusing to take any money for it."

Albert had to admit that when someone put it like that ... Pushing his rising ego down, he said, "It was Rex here who scared off the killers on both occasions. He's the one you need to thank."

Rex wagged his tail. "*I take all major forms of food if you feel like giving tribute.*"

Jean laughed. "Well, I'm thanking you anyway, Albert, but there is a meal waiting for Rex and our place is just around the corner."

Just around the corner was a little more than a mile by Albert's reckoning, but the journey didn't take long. The Schweiger's lived in an impressive two storey detached place with an open front yard and an expansive drive that led to a double garage. Similarly sized properties filled the street, all of them built pre-war, Albert judged from the designs. He spotted tennis courts behind some of the houses and a range of up-market cars to further display the wealth of the residents inhabiting them. They hadn't passed the spot where Erich was attacked, but Albert suspected it would not be far from their current location.

Every city has a most expensive postcode, so there was no reason why Antwerp would be any different. It made Albert wonder what Jean did for a living. Whatever it was, his wage combined with whatever Franka earned as a lawyer was bringing in enough money to keep the wolves from their door. Albert kept his thoughts to himself until Jean opened the front door and welcomed him inside.

"You have a beautiful home."

"Thank you. We have been very lucky."

Albert suspected they had made their own luck.

Rex sniffed the air to confirm he was now in Endal's place. The dog in question appeared in the hallway ahead a moment later, appearing through a door with a waft of delicious dinner smells.

Albert unclipped Rex's lead. "Go on, boy. Go make friends."

Endal grinned goofily. *"Chased anyone else today?"*

"Not since this morning. I did get mobbed by pigeons though."

"Oh, those guys are the worst."

Albert watched Rex follow Endal and was about to go with him when Franka appeared.

"Albert, I'm so glad you could join us."

"Thank you for your hospitality. It's very generous of you."

"Not at all. It's the least I can do. Besides, I've done a little digging and I have some information about Dirk De Graaf that might interest you."

Chapter 19

The old factory on the eastern outskirts of the city was a far cry from the plush offices of Midas Enterprises or his palatial house in the Schipperskwartier area of De Leien, the most expensive postcode in Antwerp. It was also unusual to find himself there, but he'd left his lieutenants to carry out what he felt were very simple instructions and so far they had completely failed.

Albert Smith had vanished if Medhi and Billal's report was to be believed. He was no longer at the police station, but had not returned to his hotel room where they both waited patiently to arrange a little 'accident' for the annoying old man. His dog would simply be lost in the city. Dirk might be ruthless, but he wasn't about to condone killing a dog.

Matthias and Jonas had likewise failed to finish off Erich Jannings who now had private security watching over him courtesy of his daughter and due to their botched attempt to infiltrate his room. They claimed to have never even got to the room and that the same dog from the previous evening chased them through the hospital. It was a good thing for them that the dog story turned out to be true and not some lame excuse. Despite that he was beginning to think of them as one of the loose ends he might have to tie up.

He thought he was still safe. At least he told himself he was. It was easy to become panicked by the recent events and the danger they represented, but if he could plug the gaps, there was no reason why he couldn't continue to operate where he was. The alternative was to shut everything down, to liquidate his stocks as quickly as possible, and to vanish.

He'd done it once, he could do it again. He dropped everything in a heartbeat twenty-three years ago, leaving behind his wife and child for it was that or face serious jail time and all the subsequent restrictions that would follow. They would never have let him back on a trading floor if he'd been convicted and he'd known they were getting close. So close he even knew the name of the lead FBI agent on his case.

However, the time to run was not yet upon him. Not when he had so much to lose.

The man hanging from the girder above their heads, his toes barely touching the floor, groaned and whimpered. He was bright enough to know his time had come, but also dumb enough to hope he might be rescued or find some way to escape if he just resisted for a little while longer.

Selecting a new tool from the bench, Dirk walked back over to the dangling private investigator.

"I grow bored of this conversation, Mr De Waele, so I am going to ask you one last time. What do you know about Kurt Berger?"

His voice strained, Harold De Waele had to blurt his words between gasps, "I already told you! I've never heard that name before!"

"Yet you were in Laakdal poking around in my past. Why were you there?"

"Standard investigation stuff. The Poelvoordes hired me. They wanted me to find out who destroyed their business and when I tracked the leads to find you, they wanted me to find other ... victims." Harold wished he'd crafted the sentence more carefully; suggesting the man torturing him had victims felt like an accusation that might cause offense.

"And that led you to Laakdal?" Dirk did not for one moment believe a word the P.I. was saying. There had to be more to it than complete chance.

"It did! It did! But I didn't hear anyone say the name Kurt Berger, I swear! I don't know anything."

"Sorry," Dirk shrugged. "I don't believe you."

Leaving Matthias to finish the job and deal with De Waele's body, Dirk turned away. It was possible that De Waele didn't know anything, but he wanted to be sure and the only way to do that was to send someone to Laakdal. He had to plug the gaps.

He also needed to deal with Patrick and Lubna Poelvoorde. They lost their firm when a subsidiary firm he owned through a dummy corporation bought half of their stock and shorted it – an obvious move on his part and so blind of them that they didn't see it coming. Their firm was failing and they needed money, so to stay afloat they agreed to taking on a new partner.

Dirk had no interest in their firm, it was failing for a reason, but the factory nestled on the banks of the river, the factory in which he now stood, that was a whole different subject. When he shorted the stock, he killed the business and made the couple bankrupt. They were already borrowing from the banks who saw the stock value plummet and called the loans. They couldn't pay, so the firm became his by default. He made a pile of money shorting the stock, more when he sold off all the equipment, and was due to sell the factory and the land upon which it sat for eight million Euros in the coming weeks. Had the Poelvoordes shared half a brain between them, they would have done the same thing the moment their firm started to go downhill, but a sense of duty to Patrick's grandfather, who started the firm almost a century earlier, denied them the ability to think commercially.

They lost everything and that should have been that. Yet broken and bitter, they hired a budget basement private investigator to find out who was behind it all. Dirk was forced to admit the man had done a good job. He ought not to have been able to find out as much as he apparently had, but Dirk told himself it was good news. He was identifying gaps that would now be plugged.

The remaining concern was who else might know something. Had De Waele looked far or hard enough he would have found the other 'victims'. There were plenty of them out there and Dirk needed to know if De Waele's investigation had led to any of them.

Regardless, the Poelvoordes had caused him enough strife so the clean sweep action in Laakdal would return via their hometown of Bekkevort to scoop them from their hovel. He wanted to look them both in the eye before he killed them.

The sound of a door banging closed echoed through the old factory, Medhi and Billal reacting instantly, their eyes locked on the only access point an intruder could use to get to them. Each had drawn their weapons, Glock 17 generation 4s, not stun guns this time, but it was Jonas and Matthias who strolled through the door, not the police or anyone else.

Dirk wiped his hands on a small towel which went into a black sack. Soon it would be joined by the plastic wrap coating the floor around Harold De Waele, his clothes, his belongings, and anything else that could contain the slightest scrap of evidence to link them to his body when it was found.

He waited patiently for Matthias and Jonas to come to him, such was the balance of power.

"We placed the tracker just like you said, Mr De Graaf," reported Jonas. He'd lost the coinflip and had to do the talking. "If he comes back for his things we should be able to follow where he goes."

"Good," Dirk replied, his voice devoid of emotion.

Chapter 20

Jean served dinner, a hearty beef stew called Carbonnade Flamande which he explained was a Belgian speciality. Braised in beer, the dish was sumptuous and the meat melted on the tongue. Served with creamy mashed potatoes and a trio of winter vegetables, it was as hearty a meal as Albert's empty stomach could have hoped for.

Franka was good enough to share what she knew, diving straight into the subject before her husband could even get the plates to the table.

"He's sixty-one years old, grew up in Laakdal, a small town to the east, where his parents worked blue collar jobs. He studied at Ghent University where he appears to have struggled – he scraped through his degree – but after leaving formal education he seems to have thrived. He spent some time in America and was at the World Trade Centre on September 11th, 2001. He survived, obviously, but so far as I could see he returned home almost immediately after."

"9/11," Albert commented, "That would have shaken anyone."

"I would imagine he lost a lot of friends and colleagues." Franka paused to take a bite of her meal, carefully using her knife to guide food onto her fork.

Guiltily, Albert realised he was watching her, a morbid curiosity demanding he learn how a blind person manages such mundane, daily tasks such as eating. Snatching his eyes back to his own plate before Jean noticed, Albert stuffed a forkful into his own mouth and found something neutral to look at.

Jean had 'borrowed' Endal's dinner bowl to feed Rex dinner and knew well enough to distract Franka's dog with a treat before doing so – dogs can get tetchy about sharing their most prized possession.

It had taken Rex all of about ten seconds to clear his portion of meaty chunks, commenting on the quality with a big belch when he lifted his head. Now the dogs were in the living room where they could snooze in front of a real fire and were clearly content since neither was trying to get into the dining room to beg for seconds.

Clearing her mouth and using a napkin to dab at her lips, Franka continued to report her findings.

"In the States Dirk worked for a firm called Bryant Investments. It was located on the ninetieth floor of the north tower, just a couple of floors below where the first plane hit. The owner, Phil Bryant, was killed that day along with more than half of his employees. Sorry, this is a rather morbid topic for dinner conversation, would you rather we leave it until later?"

"No, I'd like to continue." Albert looked at Franka's husband. "If that's okay with Jean."

"Of course," he replied. "We must get to the bottom of what happened to Erich."

Franka sipped her wine and dabbed her lips again.

"I could find nothing about Dirk De Graaf's escape from the building and it could be that he simply wasn't there that day."

"Your father was also a stockbroker, was he not?" Franka had already told him that was the case. "And he worked in America for a time. Is there any chance he knew Dirk from his time there."

Franka had to clear her mouth before answering. "I had the same thought myself, but I don't think that is the case. My father was only in New York for three years and he left in the mid-eighties. Dirk didn't take his job in New York until 1992. There is a theoretical possibility that they met somewhere else; it cannot be ruled out, but they worked for different firms at different times, so the likelihood is doubtful."

Albert considered that for a moment. His plate was almost empty, so he cleared the last few morsels and set his knife and fork back on the plate while considering his next question.

"Is there anything else you learned about him?"

Franka was slower with her food and unable to see the final pieces to scoop them. Jean gently took her knife and fork to load them up, passing both back into her hands so she could finish with dignity. Albert observed in silence, admiring the married couple's easy grace.

When her final mouthful was done, and Jean rose to collect the plates, she delivered another piece of information that teased Albert's curious mind.

"He has no living relatives."

"No siblings? No uncles, aunts or cousins?" Albert queried. That the parents of a man in his sixties had passed wasn't anything unusual, but the way Franka announced the news made him think there was more to it.

"He had a sister. She died two days after his parents. They were both killed in early 2002 when their house caught fire. Dirk's younger sister was killed in a hit and run accident on her way home leaving two young children and a husband. I wasn't sure what to make of it."

Neither did Albert but it felt a lot like the deaths, so close together, were related. The deaths could be nothing more than tragic accidents that occurred a few days apart. It could even be that Dirk's younger sister was too distracted by the loss of her parents to see the car before she stepped in front of it.

Or, Albert argued with himself, they were both murders. If he looked at it from that angle, and kept in mind that Dirk De Graaf was a criminal, it became conceivable that he was severing ties.

But why?

Jean arrived from the kitchen with a fresh bottle of wine. Albert thanked him for his generosity, but declined. He didn't mind wine and the Schweigers bought the good stuff, but any more alcohol would dim his senses and he wanted to be able to give Franka's case his full attention.

Franka declined too, and disappointed, Jean took the bottle back to the kitchen.

"What about Kurt Berger?" Albert prompted. "At first I thought it to be a German name, but it could easily be American. Is he someone your father knew?"

Franka pursed her lips. "I'm not sure." She was deep in thought for a few seconds before saying, "We could look through dad's things. He has photo albums and journals in the boxes we moved from his house. It's all in the annex," she explained pushing back from the table. Turning her face to the side, she called, "Endal."

Chapter 21

R ex followed Endal who led Franka through the house to a separate wing that many would label as a granny annex – a place an elderly relative moves into when living alone becomes a challenge.

"Mum died five years ago," Franka explained, leading Albert into her father's rooms. "He's yet to admit it, but I think he is happier here even though he didn't want to leave the house they lived in together for so many years. He still lived in Germany and was getting lonely."

Albert understood what that was like.

Marvelling at how easily she found her way around, Albert noted that the house was laid with different carpets in every room. He'd thought it was an odd thing to do until he realised it gave Franka the ability to know where she was. Transitioning from one room to the next provided a different texture under her feet and in the hallways a central strip of rug kept her on a straight path. She used the walls for support, one hand out to add guidance, but her other hand was latched onto Endal's harness, the broad-shouldered dog able to understand a plethora of complex commands to get her where she wanted to go.

Jean was going to follow in a few moments when he'd finished tidying after dinner, but Franka had a pretty good idea where to find what she was looking for anyway.

"They should be somewhere in that area," she wafted her free hand at the wall to Albert's right.

Erich's annex consisted of four rooms: a bedroom, a bathroom, a living space, and an extra room that served no real purpose other than as storage. There were boxes piled along one side, each of them labelled to make identifying the contents easy.

Picking one which claimed to contain albums, Albert struggled with the weight, but carried it back to the living area. Depositing it on a coffee table, he had to tear at the tape to get it open.

There were twenty or more photo albums inside and he'd spotted two other boxes marked as containing the same thing. Erich had liked to take pictures. Thankfully they were organised and labelled, the year the pictures inside were taken listed on the spine. Inside, each picture had a date and location and most had the names of those present as well.

"Anything I can help with?" asked Jean, joining them. He had a glass of wine in his hand despite no one else wanting one.

"Albert is going through the photo albums, darling. He's hoping to find a picture of Kurt Berger; you know how he liked to label all his pictures so he could remember people. You can help with that. I'm afraid I'm not much use."

Her comment prompted Albert to ask a question that had been tickling his mind since he arrived at their house.

"How did you find all the information about Dirk, Franka?"

"You mean how could I when I am blind?" she grinned to let him know she was just teasing. "I have a braille adapted keyboard and my computer talks to me. There are lots of modern adaptations for the vision impaired."

"Or the outright blind," Jean remarked, needing to duck when his wife threw a cushion directly at his head to prove her other senses were compensating just fine.

"I was born like this," Franka explained, even though Albert hadn't asked. "It's just one of those things. I've never been able to see, so I don't miss it."

Albert reached the end of the album he held and moved to the next. Each had between twenty and thirty pages, each page holding four photographs though there were also some cut smaller and fitted in around the larger ones. He had to give each one enough time to be sure he wasn't going to miss the one crucial picture that showed the man in question.

If he was even in there. If Kurt Berger even existed.

An hour later they were running out of albums, and the task, which wasn't exactly interesting to start with, had become monotonous. The dogs were spread across the carpet, both snoring their indifference to the human activity.

Closing another album with a snap that made Franka jump and earned Jean a scowl, he asked, "What about his business cards?"

"Business cards?" Albert repeated.

"Yeah, I saw them once. Erich had hundreds of them in holders, all organised alphabetically. Maybe this Berger fellow will be in there somewhere."

"Or maybe one of dad's old acquaintances will remember him," Franka offered.

Jean put down the album he held and walked back to the annex's spare room from where the sounds of rummaging soon emerged.

Albert was past ready to quit looking at photographs but there was less than half a box remaining. It would have helped if they'd been able to narrow down their search range, but that would require knowing something more about the elusive Kurt Berger.

Since Erich confused him with Dirk De Graaf, he could surmise that Kurt would be a similar age and therefore in his early sixties, but Erich's Alzheimer's dictated he approach such assumptions with caution. Erich could have seen in Dirk a man he knew forty years earlier and who was now dead. For that reason alone he pressed on through each album, reading the captions and hoping he might find the man he wanted.

"Got them," announced Jean, returning to the room with a handful of A6 sized leather-bound wallets.

Albert looked up to see what they were. He'd never really bothered with business cards and had never had one himself though he knew his children all carried them now. It was modern policing practice to hand them out to witnesses; they were more likely to make contact if it was made easy for them to find the number.

The wallets contained plastic sleeves loaded with business cards. It was just as organised as the photo albums; the output of a tidy mind.

Leaving Jean to the task of scanning credentials, Franka woke Endal.

"Endal, please fetch my phone, sweetie."

Incredibly, Endal levered herself off the carpet and left the room. Albert marvelled, unable to look back down so he could see if the dog returned with it.

Rex had lifted his head too, raising it an inch from the floor to watch his new pal depart.

"Why can't you do that?" Albert asked him.

Rex chose to respond with an expulsion of gas from his back end; he felt that was comment enough, but lying his head back down, he grumbled, "*I can, but like most other dogs I chose not to. Humans are lazy enough without us doing even more for you.*"

Endal trotted back into the room, a mobile phone clasped between her lips. It was twice the size of Albert's with chunky buttons rather than a touch screen. Endal took it right to Franka, placing her head in her lap so she could take it from her mouth.

She got a scratch around her ear and a, "Thank you," which seemed to end the transaction. She returned to her spot on the floor, flopping down with a thump in a manner only a dog can achieve.

Finally returning his gaze to the album spread across his lap, Albert's eyes alighted on a group picture. Twenty men in suits with eighties wide shoulders and even wider lapels were captured in front of a window looking out over what he guessed to be the New York cityscape. They had to be high up inside it, many floors above the ground.

The caption beneath it was 'Ready for the trading floor' and beside it '1985'. None of that really registered because Albert was staring at the man standing next to Erich.

There were no names to identify the people shown as there would be if there were just a small handful, but there was no mistaking the identity of the man to Erich's left. He was much younger, Albert placed his age somewhere around his mid-twenties, but the hairstyle, jawline, and sparkling blue eyes shone out from the six by four picture.

He'd just found Dirk De Graaf.

Chapter 22

"**A**nd I've found Kurt Berger!" Jean almost leapt out of his seat to show the business card he'd just found. "It's an old card, a plain white thing, and the area code looks wrong."

Albert had the album in his hands, open at the right page when he crossed the room to see what Jean had to show him.

Rex and Endal looked up, but neither could grasp the concept of the written word or the idea of photography. When shown a picture, they would sniff it, confirm it didn't smell of anything much, and thereafter ignore it. They were watching now only because the humans, after more than an hour of barely moving, were suddenly animated.

Jean did indeed have a business card with the name, Kurt Berger emblazoned across the front. It showed just the one number to remind everyone just how recently mobile phones came into use, and no email address. Seeing it Albert understood how Jean had been able to identify its age so easily.

The address beneath the number was for the business at which he worked: Blench and Jones Fund, the same one that employed Erich Jannings during his tenure in the States. Not exactly definitive proof, but close enough for Albert to believe the two men knew each other.

Combined with the picture he held showing Erich standing next to Dirk De Graaf, they had a triangle of connections. It meant one thing for sure: that Kurt Berger existed. Unfortunately, it did nothing to change the worry that Erich was having a senior moment when he incorrectly identified Dirk as Kurt.

"So what now?" asked Jean, the euphoria of finding that which they sought ebbing away.

"I need some numbers," said Franka. "If they worked at the same firm, and the business card indicates it was the mid-eighties ..."

Jean questioned, "Why not earlier?"

"Because Dirk would have been too young," Albert supplied the answer. "If he's sixty-one now, he would have been twenty-two in 1985. Erich left the states that year, am I right?" he checked with Franka who gave a nod. "So, it has to be between 1983 and 1985. Any earlier and Dirk would have been too young and still at university. The date next to their photograph is 1985. Kurt might be in it too, but we won't know until we track down a picture of him."

"Anyway," Franka cut in again, "I need some numbers. I think we can call around some old contacts of dad's asking who remembers Kurt Berger."

A frown knitting his brow, Jean asked, "What for? I thought the issue was with Dirk De Graaf?"

Once again it was Albert who fielded the question. "To arm us with information. Kurt Berger might have nothing to do with anything, but your father-in-law named him as the man who perpetrated the attack last night and I want to know why."

Albert removed the picture with Dirk De Graaf next to Erich and continued to wend his way through the albums looking for any further evidence. Hope there might be a photograph naming Kurt Berger kept him going until he had exhausted every last page of pictures, but he was out of luck.

Franka made phone calls, dialling numbers for old friends of her dad's, the names she recalled him talking about over the years. Some had come to the house to visit, but many were as old if not older than her father and she was only getting a one in four hit. The rest were dead or unavailable.

Jean made a pile of all the business cards he found for the men (no women) working at Blench and Jones Fund. There were twenty-eight of them and most of the cards were the same age as Kurt's if the lack of email and mobile number were anything to go by. That made absolute sense since Erich left them in 1985.

Jean had been spot on with the area code, proving it with his laptop. First introduced in 1947, they were changed and added to as more and more homes embraced the new technology. They had changed again the previous year, but pertinently new ones had been added to further divide the New York suburbs in 1984.

Clearly Kurt's business card was issued before the change in 1984, but it was for a firm that no longer existed. Blench and Jones Fund went belly up in the wake of 9/11, a detail Jean found almost as soon as he typed the name into the search bar on his laptop.

Franka continued to make phone calls with Albert reading names from the contacts list and then the numbers if it was a name Franka recognised.

Meanwhile, Jean switched to looking for Kurt Berger, but none of the people he found on the internet matched who they were looking for. Even though they didn't know his age, they could guess he wasn't in a grunge rock band, and the Kurt Berger posing with a surfboard and ripped abs probably wasn't the one they wanted either.

Drawing a blank with him, Jean moved on to the other men at the firm. Most of them didn't appear either and he realised why when he found Jacob Tanner. Now the senior hedge fund manager at Goldblat and Parker, his bio mentioned that he was a 9/11 survivor. So many of his former colleagues had no profiles because they never made it out of the building that day. They died before online professional profiles became a thing.

Raising his hand while still staring down at his laptop, he said, "I might have something here," and proceeded to explain about Jacob Tanner.

Franka insisted she would make the call, stating that it was her father the man would remember.

He and Jean listened, saying nothing when the call went through, and they held their breaths hoping this might lead to something. They had the name of the firm where Jacob Tanner worked, and they knew who they wanted to talk to. It was business hours on the US east coast, so it was reasonable to expect to be able to speak to him.

However, according to Franka, stockbrokers were not the kind of people who kept regular hours or could be expected to be in an office at any given time of the day. As senior hedge fund manager Jacob was more likely to be office bound than the people working beneath him, but it was still even odds whether she would get him first try or not.

"Goldblat and Parker, to whom shall I address your call?" Franka's phone was on speaker so Albert and Jean could hear the man's clipped voice at the other end. It was educated and professional, the New York accent there, but one which anyone would identify as well bred.

"This is Erich Jannings calling for Jacob Tanner," she used her father's name in the hope Jacob would recognise it and be more likely to take the call.

"One moment please."

They waited, the seconds ticking by with no indication if they would get to talk to the man they wanted. Jacob might know nothing, and he might possess a vital snippet of detail they needed to move to the next step. Only by quizzing him could they find out. If they drew a blank they could move on, but they only needed to speak to one person if that one person had the answers.

The clipped voice returned. "Putting you through now."

Chapter 23

J acob's face was thoughtful when he put the phone down. He hadn't heard the name 'Erich Jannings' in almost forty years and was shocked he would even be alive still let alone calling him out of the blue. He took the call only because Erich helped him when he was a rookie on the trading floor. Unlike most in their profession, Erich was willing to share what he knew and give up some of his time, which everyone knew was their most precious commodity, to develop the firm's juniors.

It wasn't Erich on the phone though, but his daughter. He had a vague half memory of the blind teenager, but his memory refused to supply a face to go with the name when she revealed her identity and apologised for the subterfuge.

She wanted to know about Kurt Berger and Dirk De Graaf, but Jacob only knew the first of them. Franka was surprised to learn he'd never heard of Dirk De Graaf and claimed she had a photograph of him standing next to her father at the firm in which they all worked.

Jacob wondered how she knew who was in the picture given her inability to see it, but not wanting to raise the point chose to brush over it. He did know Kurt Berger, but before they got into that he felt it necessary to ask a question.

"Why the sudden interest in a junior trader your father knew almost four decades ago?" Jacob believed he had good reason to want to know and suspected he was shortly to deliver news Franka would not want to hear.

"Well, it's a little complicated, but my father was stabbed yesterday evening."

Looking back at their conversation now, Jacob wished he hadn't asked if she was kidding. It was insensitive and made him sound stupid.

"I'm afraid I'm deadly serious and I fear Kurt Berger may be involved."

Jacob's forehead had folded in on itself at that point and he'd been about to deliver a response when she started talking again.

"My father is in hospital and should make a recovery, but he is yet to regain consciousness. You will want to know why I suspect Kurt Berger could be involved and the answer is because he named him."

"Named him?"

"That's right, Mr Tanner. He said, 'It was Kurt Berger'."

"That's not possible."

"Why not?"

Jacob recalled the rush of adrenaline the conversation brought. When it ended, he had left his desk to fetch the decanter of five-hundred-dollar bourbon from the cabinet in the corner of his office. His wife disapproved of his need to spend large sums on what was essentially expensive gut rot, but he paid her no attention. She was a wealthy woman because he allowed her to be, so she could put up with his vices. Despite that, he kept it at the office where she wouldn't see.

The first glass went down in a single gulp, two fingers of the dark liquid burning a path through his body. He let it settle, leaning on the edge of his desk before going back to get a second. He had a call to make.

There was a very simple reason why Kurt Berger hadn't stabbed Erich Jannings. The same reason why he couldn't have anything whatsoever to do with the crime: He was dead.

"He's what?" Franka blurted, failing to hide her surprise.

"Dead. He was in the north tower when it fell." Jacob let silence rule for several seconds before adding, "I'm afraid your father was either misheard or misunderstood. Kurt Berger has been dead for twenty-three years."

Chapter 24

A stunned silence filled the room, Albert unwilling to look up while he gathered his thoughts. The announcement pointed a big finger right in his direction. He was so sure Erich had said the name 'Kurt Berger' and perhaps he had, but if that was the case it made it all the more likely he was having a senior moment.

Drawing in a slow breath, Albert leaned back into his chair. "This changes things a little."

"Could you have been wrong about what you thought you heard?" Jean posed the question carefully, accusing Albert, but not doing so outright.

Albert lifted one shoulder, starting to shrug as he sought words to match his thoughts. Franka got in first.

"No, I think Albert heard my father correctly. Kurt Berger was a real person and my father worked with him. I doubt it could be coincidence, but equally I think we can put this down to my father's condition. Just like his confusion with Dirk De Graaf, he thought he saw someone he knew, someone from his past, but that isn't the case."

"So what do we do now?" asked Jean, sounding defeated.

"Well," Albert scratched his chin. "Dirk De Graaf is still up to something. There are still people out to hurt your father, and we still need to figure out why he was attacked. In many ways it helps us to take Kurt Berger's name off the list of suspects. It allows us to focus our interest on just one man: Dirk De Graaf."

Jean scrunched his face, struggling to comprehend. "But Dirk De Graaf is a respected businessman and philanthropist. He is known for his charity work. He's like the Bruce Wayne of Antwerp; a rich guy who helps people out."

"Then let us hope he doesn't wear a cape at night and drive a cool car because I can assure you he does have Batman's darker side." Albert went on to explain his interaction, the empty office at the very top of the city's plushest office building, his goons, and their willingness to stun an old man and his dog.

It shocked them.

"And you are the one who ended up being arrested?" Jean couldn't believe that what he was hearing could be true.

"Ah," Albert cringed. "Yes, well I bent a couple of rules, shall we say. My arrest was inevitable, but the police could be on his payroll."

Jean threw his arms in the air – Albert's story was getting more fanciful by the second.

"I'm not saying they are," Albert defended his claims. "Only that some of them might be. It means we must tread carefully and calling for help could be fraught with danger."

Sensing that her husband was becoming agitated, Franka cut in. "What's our next move, Albert? Should we dig a little deeper into Antwerp's premier businessman?"

Albert bit one corner of his bottom lip. Erich was safe for now, the security he convinced her to hire would keep her father safe, but the same could not be said for her.

"I think we should visit his hometown. I want to know more about him."

Jean would be safe enough at work; during the course of the evening Albert had learned that Jean was a pharmaceutical chemist with his own firm. It explained how they afforded the opulent surroundings and expensive postcode, but more importantly meant he would be out of the city and surrounded by people tomorrow. The same could not be said for Franka. That she was blind made her an even easier target for she would not see an attack coming.

Whether there was anything to learn about Dirk in his hometown of Laakdal, Albert could only guess, but he was curious about the death of his parents and sister. It happened more than twenty years ago, mere months after he would have returned from America following 9/11, and there might be nothing to it. Yet something about how convenient it was made Albert's senses twitch.

Dirk De Graaf was mistaken for someone else and there were no living relatives who could identify him ... did that mean something? There had to be old friends though, people who saw him after he returned to Belgium.

Tired, Albert fought to suppress a yawn and announced his intention to leave. Franka immediately offered him a spare bedroom in the main part of the house, which Jean seconded and Albert had to fight to turn down.

He wanted some time to think and needed to exercise Rex. Thanking them for their hospitality, and suggesting Franka should check in with the security firm regarding her father, he set off back to his hotel.

Chapter 25

When her husband leaned out of the house to tell her there was a call waiting, Margaret Bloomfield almost dismissed answering it. Almost. She was tending to her rose trees, a task she ought to have completed months ago and needed to finish now that she had started.

"Who is it?" she asked, wondering who would call their landline and not her cell.

Margaret's husband was already heading back into the house. It was game day and he had no desire to miss the fourth quarter. His voice drifted back out, "Some lady called Andrea Maple."

Margaret straightened her back which protested from being bent over for so long.

"Andrea Maple?" she repeated the name. It wasn't familiar, which is to say she couldn't put a face to it, but somewhere in the recesses of her mind she knew that she knew it. Putting her secateurs down with a huff and a grumble, she abandoned the rose trees and made her way inside.

The house phone was out of its cradle and lying on the kitchen counter. She could not recall the last time she had used it.

"This is Margaret Bloomfield," she held it to her ear and waited for the person at the other end to reply. Would she know who it was when they spoke? Was it an old friend with a new last name? Did she know any Andreas?

"Agent Bloomfield?"

"Not anymore. I retired several years ago. Who is this, please?" That the woman at the other end addressed her as Agent Bloomfield told her she was someone from her past, but the name still wasn't ringing any bells and the voice was just as unfamiliar.

"This is Andrea Maple, but you would know me as Andrea Berger."

Margaret turned the name around in her head a few times, trying hard to place it.

"I was married to Kurt Berger."

Recognition dropped into place like an anvil landing, the reverberations from it sending shockwaves through Margaret's body.

Blurting her words, she snapped a question, "Have you heard from him?"

"Not exactly."

A tingle of nerves had settled into Margaret's belly and her heart thumped in her chest. A successful FBI agent, it wasn't long after leaving the academy that a mentor identified her acumen for financial crimes. Two decades later she ran her own team and was known through the bureau.

Kurt Berger was a strange anomaly; a case she never solved yet was closed when he was listed among the 9/11 victims. So many of the bodies from that day were never found it caused speculation there had to be some among them who chose to abscond, leaving their spouses, their debts, and troubles behind for a new life somewhere else.

But Kurt Berger's body had been found. He was one of those tragic souls who leapt to their deaths to avoid the heat, flames, and choking smoke in the upper floors. That in itself was odd though. He worked in an office below the plane strike and though the destruction impacted their floor, most of the people working there had been able to get out.

Why couldn't he?

There were simple answers to the conundrum: he was cut off by falling debris, he was injured and couldn't escape, or maybe he was visiting another firm on a different floor when the tragedy occurred.

They would never know, but the question of his status, though officially recorded as dead, remained open in Margaret's mind for one very simple reason: His wife said it wasn't his body.

It was identified by his watch and wallet, both of which were still on his remains when they were recovered. It was even his suit, but his face was unidentifiable and his right forearm and left hand were never found. It was convenient because there was no way to use his fingerprints to confirm the body's identity. Also, his right arm didn't make sense. Severed at the elbow joint, his suit jacket was somehow intact as though he had lost his arm and then chosen to put his jacket on before jumping to his death.

Margaret knew all this because she had been on her way to arrest him on September 11th. Had she arrived an hour earlier, she and her team might well have died in the north tower along with all the other people who couldn't get out before it fell. As it was they got to the World Trade Centre twenty minutes after the second plane hit.

Weeks later she was still waiting to confirm Kurt Berger's status and went to see his body when it was identified. In the wake of the terrorist attack, the concern of an FBI agent and her investigation into insider trading was of little interest to anyone. Her objections were dismissed and the case got closed.

Kurt Berger was dead.

Yet Margaret Bloomfield never fully accepted the verdict. There were too many loose ends and unresolved anomalies. So she stayed in contact with his widow, hoping he might one day resurface. They had a two-year-old daughter in 2001. If he was out there, could he resist checking in on her?

Responding to Andrea's reply, she asked, "What does 'not exactly' mean?"

Andrea Maple explained about the call from Jacob Tanner and the call he received that prompted it. He was Godfather to the daughter she had with Kurt and after his death they stayed in touch for many years. He even attended the wedding when she remarried, sitting with her daughter for the day.

His call dredged up the past and long forgotten emotions she would much rather have never felt again. The pictures Agent Bloomfield showed her were not of her husband's body. It was battered almost to the point of being unrecognisable, but she only needed to see his skin to know it wasn't Kurt.

Kurt had very little body hair and the man in the pictures was the exact opposite: hairy like a gorilla. That didn't mean her husband was alive, but it cast a doubt over his death.

Agent Bloomfield had showed her the evidence against her husband. It was compelling and it provided a reason why he might choose to run. She had long suspected he was hiding things from her, so the news of his insider trading explained a great deal. It didn't shock her to learn his wallet and watch were found on the body of another man, but if he was out there, where was he?

That was the challenge Margaret had faced, and with his case closed her only option was to pursue it in her own time. But there was a planet to search and fresh cases on her desk. There was never a trail to follow.

Until now.

Ten minutes after her call from Andrea Maple ended, Margaret Bloomfield had a flight to Antwerp booked and was packing her suitcase.

Chapter 26

The call came in the middle of the night, waking Dirk from his sleep. His wife lifted her head when he flicked on his beside light and he quickly turned it off again with an apology.

Fumbling his reading glasses onto his head, he stared at his phone.

The number displayed on the screen wasn't one he knew, and the lack of name associated with it might have made him dismiss it under any other circumstances. But the 01-dialling code prefix denoted the call was coming from America and that was enough to send a chill through his gut.

Padding quietly from the bedroom, he snagged a towelling robe from the back of the door and wished he could have located his slippers because the underfloor heating had cycled off and the floor was like ice beneath his feet.

In any other week, the call would have been a surprise. This week it was almost expected. It also felt like another nail in his coffin.

The call rang off before he could get far enough away from his wife to answer it. He would rather not have the conversation anywhere in his house, but the situation was developing too fast. The net was closing and he had to know how long he had and whether anyone knew the truth or if, as he prayed, they were just guessing.

Settling into his home office chair, Dirk De Graaf thumbed the button to make the return call. When it ended, cold sweat coated his skin, and his hands were shaking. It was worse than he thought.

The wiretap on Andrea's house had often felt like a complete waste of money. Over the years he'd often considered cancelling the fifty thousand dollars it cost him each year, not least because he had no way to measure if they were even doing the job of listening in for the list of keywords he gave them.

Yet tonight the money invested paid for itself tenfold. He had an early warning. Already on edge from his encounter with Erich, now he knew where he stood, and it was time to go. The plan to cut and run was put in place twenty years ago, bags, money, passports and more all squirreled away so he could walk out the door in his pyjamas if he needed to.

Ingrid would be the second wife he walked away from, and should he take a third one ever, he would be a serial polygamist, a matter that concerned him not one little bit.

His heart rate slowed now that the decision was made.

But did he really need to run? In Belgium he'd built a better life than the one he had in New York. In New York he had been just another guy. He was young then, and would have climbed the ladder of success, but in Antwerp he was a big deal.

It was tempting to stay and slug it out. Oh, he would need to kill a few more people and be ready for whomever it was that came from America to investigate. But it wasn't inconceivable that he could get ahead of it. Really it boiled down to how many people suspected the truth and how quickly they could be eliminated.

Chapter 27

I n the morning, Albert awoke with a new decision in his head. He was going to stay in Antwerp and send Franka to Laakdal by herself if she was happy to go. He didn't know how she might feel about going to new places, but she had a driver and the small amount of time he'd spent with her led him to believe she was the kind of person who just got stuff done.

The driver behind his change of heart came back to his encounter with Dirk De Graaf. He pitched himself to the world as a respectable businessman, but whatever legitimate activities he might have on public display, there was no question in Albert's mind that he also had something less savoury going on in the shadows.

The man did little to hide it - what kind of high-end stockbroker nods his head to have his 'associates' stun an old man and his dog? So Albert had his sights set on digging deeper into a man who was clearly linked to whatever got Erich Janning's stabbed.

There was also the small matter of the threat to kill him. Albert held no doubt Dirk De Graaf had assigned his henchmen to perform the deed; they were dumb enough to talk about it in the elevator. The certain knowledge caused his switch in hotels and he was willing to bet they were still staking out his original room.

That being the case, Albert planned to ambush their ambush, spot where they were hiding out, and call the cops. He would be careful not to involve Bervoets – he would make no mention of Erich Jannings or the mugging, but would report a different crime, a car theft perhaps. All he needed was to get a couple of cops to his location. Then he could reveal he'd found the men behind Erich's violent attack.

That wouldn't work if De Graaf sent the middle eastern pair after him, but he figured it was an even bet and worth the risk. The brothers looked to be De

Graaf's personal protection and that being the case it would be the other pair. Unless he had more henchmen than Albert had seen so far.

He doubted their arrest would have much impact on Dirk De Graaf's movements, but it would give him the opportunity to watch what happened. Getting back inside Enterprise House was off the table, Albert doubted he would get past the revolving door before security threw him out, but he could watch the building from the market stalls in Grote Markt. It was a different angle, but no less likely to yield something than a trip to De Graaf's hometown.

Albert ran it through his head again and nodded at his decision. Having Franka with him would complicate things and factoring her into his movements and reactions would slow him down. Besides, he wanted to see if there was anything to discover in Laakdal so splitting up made sense – two birds and all that.

Rolling out of bed, he grimaced slightly at the pyjamas he wore. Though the hotel was good enough to provide all the toiletries for free, they made him buy the pyjamas which were emblazoned with the hotel's crest on the right breast. He wouldn't have minded so much, but they were not the best fit and the flannel material made him too hot.

There was no room for them in his luggage either, so it was perhaps a good thing he found them disagreeable.

Rex had been dozing for some time, his head resting on the carpet just a few feet from the bed. He tried getting comfortable in the armchair by the window, but though it was soft and yielding, it was also far too small for him to fit. No matter how he contorted his body, he simply couldn't find a way to get his backside and his head into positions that would allow him to rest comfortably.

With his human up and getting dressed, Rex stretched out his front paws and arched his back. He needed to go outside and he wanted some breakfast. Unfortunately, he already knew there was no food in their room and wasn't sure what the plan might be to resolve what he felt to be a major issue.

Albert was clean following a bath when he got back to the room the previous evening, but made sure with a wash at the sink before donning his upper layers. Teeth brushed and final remaining strands of hair dabbed into place with a little water, the first task on his list was to get Rex out and fed.

"Come on," Rex whined at the door. *"I've really got to go!"*

Looking to avoid a clean up job, Albert did precisely that, securing Rex to his lead before opening the door, and bracing himself just in case there were two hoodlums outside. There were not, and the hotel corridor was devoid of life or sound.

Outside Albert's breath formed clouds of condensing vapour which always made him feel like a human steam train. Rex tried to lift his leg on the brass post for the brocaded rope leading to the hotel entrance and had to be coaxed across the road where his um, output would be less visible.

Feeling the pressure drain away, Rex wasn't paying much attention to anything when a pigeon landed a few feet in front of his face. It was on the ground and looking at him, its head side on to eyeball him with one eye.

Rex squinted at it. *"Back for more, are you? I sure hope so, birdy, because I'm not inclined to leave the score at one nil."*

The pigeon showed no sign that it comprehended and flew off back into the sky where Rex lost sight of it.

Albert walked a circuit around the block, finding a bakery on the back leg just around the corner from the hotel. There he bought a fresh bread roll which Rex promptly inhaled. Albert was also hungry but had breakfast included with his room. More commonly staying in small privately run places, he would often take Rex to breakfast with him. He doubted the hotel would be happy with that though, registered emotional support animal or not, so he went back into the hotel room where Rex promptly jumped on the bed for a half hour snooze, and Albert found his way to the restaurant.

Quietly working his way through some fruit and yoghurt, Albert reflected on what he thought the Kurt Berger/Dirk De Graaf confusion could mean. However, the more thought he gave to the conundrum the more likely it became that Erich had simply been confused.

Except that failed to explain why De Graaf got so hot under his collar about it.

When the time ticked around to nine o'clock and Albert felt it was okay to disturb her morning, he dialled Franka's number. The phone rang enough times that he began to question if she would answer, but she did, saying, "Good morning, Albert," to a backdrop of Endal huffing and panting to remind him that the dog had to fetch it for her.

How she knew the identity of her caller was another mystery, but he guessed it would be one more clever feature of the technology designed to make her life easier.

"Good morning, Franka. Is there any news regarding your father?" Erich Jannings remained Albert's number one witness. If Franka's father regained consciousness, there was every possibility he could supply all the answers: Why he confused De Graaf with Berger, why De Graaf got so upset by the error, and why he was stabbed on his way home. He might hold the key to everything, but then again he might wake in a confused state, his foggy mind denying Albert the chance to get reliable answers. He wouldn't know until Erich was back with them.

With a sigh, Franka said, "No, I'm afraid not. Not that the doctors have provided an update since I pestered them last night. I'm having to call the security firm to get a report from their operatives. The latest is that there is no change to his condition."

It was disappointing, but no surprise. No one was saying it, but Erich was lucky to have survived the surgery and wasn't out of the woods yet. His health could yet go either way.

Moving forward, Albert got down to the business of outlining his thoughts and was surprised to hear Franka agree.

"That makes perfect sense, Albert. I will have my driver collect me within the hour and should be in Laakdal before noon."

"Super."

"What specifically is it you want me to look for?"

"I want to know if De Graaf has been back there. If people know him. How he reacted when his parents and sister died so suddenly. Was there an investigation."

"Wait, you think De Graaf might have been behind it? I know you suspect him of sending the men who hurt my father, but killing your own family? What would motivate a man to do that, Albert?"

Albert's voice was cold when he replied, "That's what I'm hoping to find out."

Chapter 28

A cross town from the De Liene district where Albert and Franka were having their conversation, Detective Filip Bervoets was not enjoying his start to the day. He worked as a homicide detective in a big city, so seeing bodies wasn't a new thing and he'd hardened against it a long time ago.

There was something about this one though that made him want to look away. The victim had clearly been tortured prior to his death and there were deep abrasions to his wrists suggesting he'd been hung by them for some time.

Anything they might have used to identify him had been removed – fingerprints, teeth, wallet, and other sundries. Even his clothes were gone. Despite that the man was identified before Bervoets arrived. Ironically the medical examiner knew him though he could not explain what Harold De Waele was doing in Antwerp or what might have brought about his terrible end.

He had an office in Bekkevort and Bervoets was going to have to go there. It changed what he had planned for the day, but that was the nature of his work. He did nothing to resist it and though he could have contacted the local police in Bekkevort, Bervoets knew he would learn more going himself. Plus the trip would get him out of the city for the day.

Walking back to his car, he wondered what the heck De Waele had been involved in to warrant such brutal treatment.

Chapter 29

One thing Albert knew he needed to do was retrieve his belongings. They were still at the Tulip Inn Hotel where he stayed the first night. It was at the lower rent end of things, but he expected to find his suitcase and backpack in his room where he'd left them.

However, the same prudent caution that necessitated alternative accommodation dictated he approach the location with stealth. He wanted to be right and to find the two men who stabbed Erich waiting for him in a car down the road. If they were there, they would be watching for him to exit the building with a plan to follow. Or it could be the other two, the ones in suits who favoured stun guns. He didn't know any names, but all four faces were indelibly etched into Albert's brain.

The same could be said for Rex though with him it was the scents which he recorded. He could recognise faces and even voices or the distinct sound of a person's footfall, but smell was by far the most accurate sense and the one he would always rely upon.

He sniffed the air in the street, drawing it into his nose where he filtered and deciphered it. He could smell a dead rat lying in the gutter twenty yards down the street, a blob of bubble gum where someone had recently stuck it on the pole at a nearby bus stop, car exhausts, breakfasts cooking, and the scents of people who had passed by in the last half an hour. It was all quite familiar and nothing to remark upon.

What he'd been searching for was any sign of the men who stunned him yesterday. Rex wasn't aware his human befell the same fate for he was already unconscious when it happened, but had he known it would only have strengthened his resolve to mete out some punishment the first chance he got. The next time he caught their scents, he was going to bite someone.

Then there was the other two, the pair who had now successfully evaded him twice. He wanted a third crack at them for sure. Everything started when they chose to stab a person. There was no trace of them though. If they were nearby, they had to be downwind of his location.

Albert stopped at a corner to watch. He denied them the chance to kill him last night, but it wouldn't be enough to put them off and De Graaf didn't strike Albert as the kind of man who gave up easily.

He watched the front of the hotel and the street facing it for fifteen minutes. They wouldn't be waiting inside; hiding in the room would corner them and they had run from his dog twice already. If they were here, they would have to be in the street.

Cars came and went, parking spaces snapped up the moment they became available. Some didn't move at all, but as the cold began to creep through the soles of his shoes and into his feet, he judged that there was no one waiting to ambush him.

Rex had grown bored and was lying at Albert's feet half asleep when the old man suddenly clicked his tongue and started walking.

Albert kept his eyes open, looking for any sign of De Graaf's associates or indeed danger of any kind. He walked right by the hotel and kept going, setting off so he had a couple of heavily built guys in construction clothes at his back. They would be on their way to a site somewhere, but having them so close behind meant no one would be able to jump out of a car and grab him or Rex.

A hundred yards past the Tulip Inn Hotel, Albert about turned, crossed the street and walked back on the other side. The process took less than five minutes and confirmed, as much as possible, that there was no one waiting for him to appear. It came as a disappointment. Partly because it meant he was wrong about De Graaf's keenness to remove him from the playing board, but also because his hope to get Erich's attackers arrested was lost.

For now, at least.

There were two people manning the small hotel's reception desk when he walked by it, both looking up and giving him a polite nod.

His room appeared just as he'd left it. That didn't mean no one had been in it because it could have been professionally tossed, but he didn't think that was the case. The men he'd met so far didn't leave him thinking finesse was their thing.

He paused for long enough to change his underpants and socks. Yesterday's were probably fine to wear again, but he would spend the day conscious he was in day-old underwear. Task complete, he closed his suitcase, slid his arms into the backpack containing the rest of his belongings, and unlocked his door.

Across town Jonas nudged Matthias' arm. Albert Smith was on the move.

Chapter 30

The drive to Bekkevort took ninety-three minutes, a third of which was spent stuck in the slow traffic in Antwerp. Mendi and Billal, brothers from Iran, had an address and a task to complete when they got there.

Neither one knew what had their boss so on edge, but he'd been acting spooked since the old man approached him in the street. Erich Jannings, whoever he was, called Dirk De Graaf by a different name. They thought it was nothing more than a confused old gaffer mistaking one person for another, yet that clearly wasn't the case.

Not that it mattered to them. They were sufficiently well paid to not care about their boss's motivations. If he wanted them to destroy an office in Bekkevort, they would do it without needing an explanation why.

In the driver's seat, Billal took a drive by the address, both men staring through the right side windows of their car to spot the office. They had the right street, but none of the businesses displayed the name they wanted.

"It must be inside," Medhi remarked, pointing at a set of glass double doors. To the left of the doors a series of letter boxes indicated there to be more than one business inside. Medhi squinted but could not make out the names in the little windows next to the flaps, however a double check of the address confirmed they were in the right place.

Billal parked the car two blocks away on a residential street where there were no cameras. They both had sunglasses, ball caps, hooded tops, and Covid style face-masks to ensure any cameras they did pass could not be used for facial recognition. Their hands were clad in black contact gloves, the kind mechanics wear to keep the muck and grease from their skin.

From the boot, Medhi collected a small toolbox, carrying it in his left hand which left his right, the more dominant, free to reach for his weapon, not that he expected to have to use it.

They were professionals, and prided themselves on being several classes above Matthias and Jonas, the two local thugs their boss employed.

Neither man saw need to speak on their way to their destination. There were people about, but not too many. Bekkevort, a small town to the east of Antwerp, was a quiet place where nothing much happened. It was close to eleven o'clock on a Thursday, so the kids were in school and the adults were working. The only people out and about were the retired, the unemployed, and mums with babies.

They passed them all by, silently making their way to the address they had for De Waele's office. The ex-cop was a nothing, a private investigator barely getting by, not that he would ever worry about his bills again. They expected his office to be a drab, little place and were not disappointed. What they hoped for, though, was to find his secretary behind the desk.

They could and would destroy the office, razing it to the ground to leave no trace of their boss's name. They would remove any hard drives and data storage devices they could find, and spend a few minutes going back through his emails to see where the name 'Dirk De Graaf' might appear. If De Waele had communicated with anyone other than the Poelvoordes they would locate and eliminate them too, but destroying the office would do nothing to remove information from the secretary's memory and for that reason they were glad to find her reading a book at her desk.

Medhi closed the door behind his brother who waved hello to the dumpy middle-aged woman when she looked up. There were blinds in the windows, the old kind that close when you twist a bar at one end. They had a thick film of dust coating one side where they hadn't been cleaned or moved in years.

"Can I help you?" the woman asked, the timbre of her voice betraying a touch of concern when Medhi blocked out the view from outside. By then it was too late and Billal was at her desk. The cosh concealed in his sleeve appeared with a flick, the secretary breathing a whimpering sigh as she sprawled across the desk and fell to the floor.

They made quick work of the office, erasing files and confirming the only place Dirk De Graaf's name appeared was on the emails back and forth to the couple who hired him. Task complete, Billal shorted out a socket in the corner by the bin making sure the sparks fell to the paper below and caught. The woman moaned, a soft cry that showed she was coming around.

Billal smeared some blood from her head wound onto the corner of a filing cabinet. It wasn't the most convincing touch, but it would be enough to cause the police to question what they were looking at.

The fire began to lick at the wall. They used no accelerants, nothing that would obviously suggest it was arson in play. It meant they had to wait long enough to be sure the fire would take and not just fizzle out, but when a flaming chunk of paper toppled from the bin and the carpet caught, they knew the job was as good as done.

With a glance through the blinds to check the coast was clear, they exited swiftly to limit the amount of smoke escaping, and left the little mall of small businesses via the glass double doors two seconds later.

Only when they were clear of the town did they remove their masks and sunglasses.

Chapter 31

Twelve kilometres to the north of Bekkevort, Franka Schweiger was arriving in Laakdal. It was not a place she had ever visited before. Nor did she anticipate having a reason to ever return. Her plan was to find out all there was to know about Dirk De Graaf as quickly as possible and return to Antwerp so she could check on her father.

Her career as a lawyer dictated research was nothing new, but this was totally different to what she was used to. When Albert suggested she tackle this part of their investigation, she had jumped at the chance, only to later question what, precisely, she was supposed to do.

She could have asked Albert, but it felt silly to do so. Surely, she could figure things out for herself.

With no living relatives in the town, there nevertheless had to be people who remembered Dirk de Graaf. In theory there was a former brother-in-law, Dirk's little sister's husband. Her kids would be adults now and for all Franka knew the husband and kids had all moved away. Not that she knew their names, that information had proven impossible to find.

All she had was a last name: Opbrouck.

Josse stopped outside the post office. He used to offer his help to get her places outside of the car, but had long since given up as Franka always claimed she could manage.

Endal had slept almost the whole journey, but awoke when the car stopped and Franka touched her shoulder.

"Come along, Endal. Time to earn your keep."

She yawned and stretched, but was ready to work when the driver came around to open the door to the pavement. Endal waited until Franka was out and had her harness firmly in her grip before setting off.

"To the post office, please, Endal."

Momentarily confused because this wasn't where they lived and it wasn't their post office, she understood sufficiently to guide Franka into the building to their front. She joined the queue and waited until a counter space became available.

Using her white stick to find the boundaries of her surroundings when a voice called, 'Next!', Franka said, "Hello," and waited for an answer.

Behind the counter, Roxane Berard had called for the next person in line while attempting to retie her ponytail. At thirty-three she had a new boyfriend, only the second since her divorce five years ago and the first in more than a year. Arriving at work with a minute to spare, an empty belly from missing breakfast, and a slight hangover from too much wine, she was bereft of makeup and had only just about managed to scrape her hair into some semblance of control behind her head.

Dropping the stupid hairband, she'd called, "Next," and slid off her stool to find it. Consequently, she didn't see the blind woman until she popped back up.

"Oh, hello."

Laakdal was small enough that Roxane saw the same people day in and day out. She knew most of their names because they were on the forms they filled in, and they knew hers because it was on her badge.

The blind woman was new.

"I'm hoping you can help me," Franka delivered the lines she rehearsed in the car. She wanted personal information and as a lawyer knew she shouldn't be able to get it. However, there were ways around that and it called for carefully posed questions. "I'm trying to locate anyone who might remember Dirk De Graaf. He used to live here, but so far as I am aware he has no living relatives. However, he did have a brother-in-law with the last name Opbrouck." Franka left the sentence in the air. Technically, she was yet to ask a question, she had merely stated what she hoped to achieve.

Roxane didn't know who Dirk De Graaf was, but she knew the Opbroucks because she went to school with Daphne. Her younger brother was the year below them.

"Do you mean Koen Opbrouck?" Roxane enquired.

"Is that the man who was married to Olivia. Her maiden name would have been De Graaf."

Roxane shrugged. "I don't know about that, but Koen Opbrouck is the father of Daphne and Kevin, and they are the only Opbroucks in Laakdal that I know of."

Thinking this was easier than expected, Franka tried another question. "Are there *any* De Graafs in Laakdal?" Perhaps there was a distant relative her research failed to identify. They might know more about Dirk or be able to point her at someone who would.

Roxane repeated the question to the woman sitting to her left. Thirty years older, Kitty was an authority on everything and everyone local.

"No. There're no De Graafs living here now. Who's asking?" She stamped the form under her nose and handed it back before looking across to see Franka in front of Roxane.

"I'm trying to locate anyone who remembers Dirk De Graaf," she repeated her earlier statement – still not a question.

"Oh, well you want to talk to the police," said Kitty.

Franka's eyebrows climbed her forehead.

"Dirk De Graaf was best friends with Thierry Belvaux when they were kids. I remember them both getting arrested for stealing a car when they were about eighteen. Thierry is the desk sergeant at the station. He's supposed to have retired, but they haven't been able to recruit anyone new in years."

Armed with a next place to stop, Franka asked Endal to take her back to the car. She hadn't learned anything yet, and maybe there was nothing to find. As Albert explained it, investigative work was a lot of looking under stones because there was no way to know which one would yield a clue. Her trip to Laakdal might be a waste of time, but feeling confident, she asked Josse to locate the town's police station.

Chapter 32

E rich was yet to regain consciousness, but it could happen at any time and there was no one better placed to explain what was going on than the man who set it all in motion. With Erich's daughter out of the city, Albert believed it fell to him to make sure her father was as the security detail reported and he wanted to check on them too.

It only occurred to him when he considered how good of a job they might be doing that no one would have passed them descriptions of Erich's attackers. Only Albert could do that and would warn them about the two middle eastern men at the same time. Having specific threat knowledge might prove vital.

Back at Hotel Palais De Le Court in the affluent De Liene region of Antwerp, Albert placed his small, blue suitcase on a table set between two chairs and shed his backpack. He was going back to the hospital and taking Rex with him was not a good idea. Not if he wanted them to let him in.

He fished Rex's water bowl out of his backpack, filled it at the sink, and placed it in the corner of the room. Albert didn't like leaving Rex behind, not least for the fact that his dog was also his protector, but it would only be for a short while.

"Now, I won't be long," Albert promised, coming down to one knee so he could give Rex a hug and look him in the eye. "Try not to get into any bother when I am out."

"*Any bother?*" Rex questioned. "*I'm going to be asleep on your bed before you get back to the street.*" He wasn't allowed to sleep on the bed and consequently did it as often as he could. The old man always caught him or knew where he'd been, but it wasn't as though he withheld Rex's biscuit ration as punishment for the transgression.

Albert rose to his feet, pushing on his knees to overcome gravity which seemed all the more powerful in recent years.

"*Before you go ...*" Rex nudged Albert's coat pocket with his nose. Getting left behind was easily enough justification for a gravy bone.

Albert couldn't help but chuckle. "Always thinking with your stomach, eh, Rex?" He fished a treat from the stash in his pocket, patted Rex on the head, and made sure the room was locked tight when he closed the door.

Confident Dirk De Graaf's men wouldn't find where he was staying, Albert made his way back to the tram stop and waited for the approaching tram. Getting around the city was easy using public transport, not like at home where a person needed to pack emergency provisions before setting out. Buses were unreliable, the train workers continually went on strike for more pay and consequently fewer and fewer people rode them which diminished the income from ticket sales that could conceivably have supported such a demand.

Of course, Albert lived in the countryside where public transport rarely roamed.

Half an hour of stopping and starting took him across the city and back to Hospital Universitair Ziekenhuis where he kept his head down through reception lest he be recognised. Thankfully, no one challenged him or even seemed to notice him amid the other patrons going to and fro.

Retracing his steps, Albert returned to Erich's room where a man in a suit with observant eyes and an unreadable expression waited outside like a sentinel.

Tall at six feet and four inches, the man filled his suit jacket with broad shoulders. Albert saw him observe the doctors and nurses going by, the patients too, assessing everyone before moving on to check the next nearest person as they approached.

When the man's eyes fell on Albert, he raised a hand to get his attention. "Hi, I'm Albert Smith," he said, knowing Franka had placed him on a list of expected visitors. "Is Erich awake?"

The security guard twisted at the waist to look through the window in the door.

"I don't think so. I haven't heard the hospital staff talking to him." His attention was only elsewhere for a split second; a quick glance to check the patient's condition and straight back to the task of watching for danger. It gave Albert confidence.

The news that Erich was still out of it was less thrilling though.

"You mind if I go in?"

The man lifted his right hand, bringing his jacket cuff close to his mouth to speak into the microphone attached to his wrist.

"Sergei I am entering the room. I need cover in the hallway."

Albert couldn't hear the reply; it came through the man's earpiece, but a carbon copy in a matching suit appeared five seconds later. He had a to-go coffee cup in his hand which he drained and ditched in a bin as he approached.

The man guarding the door nodded to Albert and pushed it open. They went inside as Sergei arrived to take up watch outside. It was slick.

The bank of monitors to the right of the bed displayed Erich's vitals: heartrate, blood oxygen saturation, more that Albert couldn't identify. It did so with nothing more than a gentle hum.

"Mr Jannings?" Albert called out, his voice a little louder than normal conversation.

The man in the bed didn't so much as twitch.

"Erich?" Albert tried again, this time getting closer.

When he tried a third time he placed a hand on his arm. Still there was no response. He was lying in a different position to the previous day, but Albert assumed the nursing staff had moved him to prevent bed sores occurring. Briefly Albert considered pinching the man's skin to see if a little pain might rouse him, but he dismissed the notion. He knew nothing about comas or whether it was possible to jolt patients into waking from them.

Ultimately, he wasn't getting any answers from the man best placed to answer them and he had to accept the situation for what it was. He had other options, other avenues to pursue, they just weren't as promising or as easy as getting the truth from Erich.

Irked, he thanked the hulking security guard and left the room.

Chapter 33

J onas and Matthias had to score a win this time. The boss was already displeased with them. Defeated by an old man and a dog twice they then failed to find them for their third attempt. Erich Jannings now had private security outside his door which was going to make dealing with him all the more difficult, but the Englishman and his dog were at a hotel in De Leien.

The App on Jonas' phone showed them the address. He'd been there for a while, the tracker in his suitcase pinpointing his position with a reasonable degree of accuracy. It didn't mean the old man was there, but that was okay. They could go through his things – old people made notes with a pen and paper. If he'd written anything down about Dirk De Graaf or Kurt Berger, whoever the heck that was, they would find it. Then they could lie in wait for him – not in his room, that would be folly, but somewhere within the hotel. A swift ambush was all it would take. One thrust with a knife and it would be done. The dog could get the same treatment for that matter regardless of De Graaf's thoughts on the subject.

The App was even clever enough to show them what floor it was on when they got close enough. At the door – the app showed the tracker as just a few feet beyond their current position – they removed hammers from their pockets. They were carrying guns, but using them would draw attention fast. They also had knives, but they made a mess that always ended up on the person holding the knife no matter how careful a person tries to be. The blood would draw attention too, so it was the blunt instrument they readied.

Rex lifted his head from the bed covers. He'd wasted no time in getting comfortable, clambering onto the bed almost before his human had the door shut. Sleep came easily, his canine brain drifting away on a cloud of contentedness until something poked him back to semi-alertness.

Employing all his senses, Rex felt his hackles rise and a low growl begin at the back of his throat – the killers were back. They were outside his door, their quiet movements and hurried whispers cutting through his slumber.

Rex got to his feet and was about to bark when he realised the natural response would give him away. The men outside were trying to get in, that much he believed to be true. Barking would only serve to scare them away. His human wasn't here so there was no need to defend the room and no one present to tell him not to bite at will.

Climbing gingerly down from the bed so he wouldn't make a thump and alert the killers to expect him, Rex considered what his best course of action might be. However, the door opened and the time to plan was gone.

A thousand generations of instinct kicked in. Rex knew precisely who he was looking at. Framed in the doorway, the two killers he'd chased and missed twice were coming into the room. Their eyes were trained across the room at head height so they didn't see Rex for the first half second and that was all he needed to gain the advantage.

A single bound took him across the room. Both men had something in their right hands, but it wasn't a knife or a gun; two things Rex knew to fear. The smaller of the two was closer, his partner still holding the door handle with a mind to close it once he was through.

Rex barrelled into Jonas, his teeth clamping over the fleshy part of his right forearm to neutralise the threat his weapon posed. He could have given a shake with his body, using his weight to pull the man off balance, but Rex chose to just keep on running.

With an arm in his mouth and a high-pitched scream bouncing around the room and out into the corridor, Rex slammed into Matthias' left leg, using the crown of his skull to ram sideways through his knee joint.

Yanked from his feet when his right arm went behind him and down, Jonas spun into Matthias, who was, himself, already tumbling to the carpet. The bodies formed a log jam in the doorframe, Jonas' arm effectively stopping Rex because he didn't possess the strength to tear it from his body.

He spat it out and turned to face the two men. He could taste blood, the red liquid seeping through Jonas' shirt to stain the fur around Rex's mouth.

They were getting up and though Rex knew he could attack again, he could also see they had abandoned their hammers and were reaching for something else – almost certainly something more deadly. He could lunge and bite one, but getting to both now the element of surprise was gone was unlikely. Disappointed he couldn't inflict more damage, Rex did the only sensible thing – he turned and ran.

Jonas, his right arm a searing ball of agony, tried to get to his gun using his left hand. With the result that he fumbled and dropped it. Matthias had withdrawn his knife. His left knee felt like it was on fire, and he wanted nothing more than to exact revenge, but the dog was racing down the corridor, heading for the stairs and only a gun would stop him now.

Snatching Jonas' dropped weapon, he aimed at Rex's back end only to see the dog turn sharp right and vanish to an accompanying squeal of surprise. A heartbeat later, a housekeeping lady with a loaded cart of fresh towels, bedding, and sundries rolled into sight. She'd come from the elevators, the dog undoubtedly going in as she came out.

Moving toward Matthias and Jonas, her gaze lingered on the space behind her for just long enough for Matthias to put his partner's gun away. When she looked back the way she was going, both men were on their feet and shuffling into Albert's room. They couldn't have given chase if they wanted to; neither was in a fit state and Matthias could barely stand on his left leg.

It was their intention to toss Albert's room, but first they had to recover and Jonas needed to dress the puncture marks in his right arm.

A third attempt to appease their boss and a third failure. Neither man voiced their thoughts, but both were thinking the same thing: It was time to get out of Antwerp.

Chapter 34

There were no direct flights from Austin, Texas to Belgium. Not one. Not ever. And there were no indirect flights to Antwerp either. Fortunately for Margaret Bloomfield there were indirect fights to Brussels and that was less than thirty miles away.

All the same it took her the whole night and a chunk of the morning to get off the plane. She was lucky to get a seat at such short notice; she knew that, but was appalled at the cost all the same. In Brussels with a small suitcase and whole lot of purpose, she then needed to rent a car to make the final leg.

With the seven-hour time difference and far too little sleep despite the business class seat she'd been forced to pay for – the only seat left on the entire plane – she felt better than she believed she had any right too. She also suspected fatigue would catch up on her soon enough.

However, her search for justice was largely to blame for keeping her awake and it was what drove her onwards now. She had crossed the Atlantic for her own sake, no one else's, and she had no authority to do anything to Kurt Berger when she found him. But find him she would, of that Margaret Bloomfield held unshakable belief.

However, while she was retired, had no badge or sidearm, no jurisdiction or power, there *were* FBI agents on European soil and when she knew where to send them, she would call in every favour she could to make sure he was arrested and returned to the states to stand trial. Not because she wanted revenge against him for getting away, and not because he was a mar on her brilliant record. No, she wanted to see him caught because he was a murderer. He had to be. How else could his clothes, wallet, and watch have ended up on another man's body?

Unless he was an opportunist and found the man already dead. Either way, lying in Kurt Berger's grave was the body of a man whose own family most likely had no idea their loved one had died. Getting to the bottom of it would give her closure in a way her husband would never understand.

He told her not to go. Said she was wasting her time and their money. Well, it wasn't *their* money, it was her pension and savings. He'd never earned enough to make a worthwhile contribution.

Her credit card was approved and the man behind the Alamo counter handed over the keys to a new model Kia. She didn't care what it was, just so long as it came with satnav that could be reprogrammed to speak English.

Margaret figured an hour to get to Antwerp, but once there she had no destination, only a name and a phone number. Franka Schweiger was the person who triggered Jacob Tanner to call Andrea Maple who in turn made the call that got Margaret Bloomfield out of Texas for the first time in ten years.

She would call her from the car and arrange to meet. Margaret was coming for Kurt Berger and the sense of excitement she felt as she checked traffic and pulled away from the airport was palpable.

Chapter 35

L ieutenant Filip Bervoets squinted through his windscreen at the emergency vehicles filling the street ahead. An angry thump on his bonnet drew his eyes to find a cop in uniform gesticulating impatiently that he needed to turn his car around. They were sending all traffic back until they could deal with whatever issue they had.

Fire was a safe bet given the engine parked diagonally across the street and the fire fighters visible around it.

Flashing his badge at the cop, he waited for the barrier to be moved and went through to park on the other side.

On the pavement, Bervoets stuck a piece of gum in his mouth and started to chew. Looking back at the beat cop, he called, "What happened?"

The cop shrugged, unwilling to divert his attention away from his task for long. "Beats me."

Setting off, Bervoets made his way toward the fire engine, noting dismally that it was right in front of the place he wanted to go. The place he drove here from Antwerp to visit. It did not bode well.

Finding the fire chief, he showed his badge again while peering through a set of smeared glass double doors. The ground around his feet was soaked, standing water coating it though it was draining away and the fire fighters were starting to pack up their gear.

"Any victims?" he asked.

"Just one. Found by her desk. Looks like she hit her head, probably while trying to put out the fire, got burned up in the process."

"Let me guess; the fire was in De Waele Investigations and the dead person is the woman who works there, right?" It was shaping up to be one of those days. First a dead former cop turned P.I. and now his assistant. Whatever De Waele had stumbled upon, someone wanted it kept secret.

The fire chief had been about to say something, his attention mostly on one of his probationary fire fighters who was goofing around and not being reeled in by the crew's lead hand. However, the accuracy of the detective's guess made him do a double take.

Frowning, he asked, "How'd you know that?"

Bervoets huffed out a tired breath. "I'm a good guesser."

"Yeah, well you got one part wrong. The woman didn't work there, she worked across the hall in a hairdressing place. The woman who does work there got called away because her kid was sick at school and she had to go take him some medicine. Something like that anyway. The victim was just covering the phone for her."

Bervoets' eyes widened in disbelief. Was the fire chief yanking his chain.

"Is she here?" he begged to know.

The fire chief pointed. "Yeah. That's her over there talking to the cops."

The woman's makeup was trashed, half of it washed away by tears and her hair was a mess, probably from yanking at it in horror and denial. The local cops, two detectives Bervoets didn't know, said they were done with her. Their questions were routine only. Taking him to one side, one of them said it looked like an accident. The coroner would make sure, but the body was too burned up for the medical examiner to make anything better than a gut assessment. There was a wound to her head, but no reason yet to suspect foul play. The fire didn't look like arson and no one burns a place up for the insurance money in the middle of the day.

Bervoets held a different opinion, but then he'd seen De Waele's remains just a few hours ago.

He introduced himself to Veerle Vandernoot, a thin woman in her mid-thirties with tobacco stains on her fingers and a nervous disposition. Given the circumstances, Bervoets guessed she was blaming herself. That was as natural as it was wrong, yet he knew nothing he could say would change how she felt right now and he was too focused on getting to the truth of things to care all that much.

Gritting his teeth, he knew he had to make her day even worse, but chose to get some answers first.

"Veerle, can you tell me what your boss was doing in Antwerp?"

She puffed on a cigarette in a hurried manner as though eager to get as much nicotine into her body as possible.

"Following a lead, I guess. Working a case. The same thing he always does." She didn't make eye contact while delivering her response, looking everywhere but Bervoets' eyes until he said nothing and waited for her to look up.

When she did, he said, "I need to know what he was investigating, Veerle. It's important. Who were his clients?"

"A couple called the Poelvoordes. Patrick and Lubna. They hired him a couple of months back to look into some big shot who made them go bankrupt. It was a total waste of money. I heard Harry explaining to them that they needed a financial analyst, but they insisted he was all they could afford. They wanted him to find other people who had suffered the same as them. They had it in their heads that they could get their money back if they could just find out who was behind it all. They borrowed money and the next thing they knew they were broke, and the lender owned their business. Now he's selling it, and they seem to think they ought to get a share."

"And that took Harold to Antwerp?"

"Harry," she puffed on her cigarette again. "He hates being called Harold."

Not anymore he doesn't, Bervoets thought to himself.

Veerle stamped out her cigarette beneath a high-heeled shoe that had seen much better days and lit another.

"Why did Harry go to Antwerp?" Bervoets pressed to get an answer.

"That's where this big shot stockbroker guy lives."

Bervoets blinked. His brain seemed to slow, like it was suddenly filled with tar. A big shot stockbroker?

"Hey," Veerle dragged hungrily on her cigarette, "why you asking me all these questions anyway? You want answers, go talk to Harry."

Sighing, Bervoets waited until she was looking his way before delivering the hammer blow.

"Harold De Waele was found dead this morning."

Veerle took it worse than he predicted, and it was ten minutes before he finally wangled from her the name of the big shot her boss was investigating. Walking back to his car, he felt perplexed and not a little bit confused.

He could have listed a thousand unlikely names Veerle Vandernoot could have said, from the Easter Bunny to Santa Clause and right the way through to Jack the Ripper, but he would never have thought to add Dirk De Graaf. Yet it was the second time in two days that the wealthy philanthropist's name had been used in conjunction with a crime. The old man from England seemed convinced he had something to do with Erich Jannings being stabbed.

Veerle couldn't recall the contact details for the Poelvoordes, but their names proved enough to track down their details. They didn't answer their house phone though, and when he dug a little deeper and found where each of them worked, Bervoets discovered neither had shown up for work today.

He did not like the way things were stacking up. He went by their house in Bekkevort, a shabby place in a run-down part of the town. There was no sign of foul play, but a single drop of blood on their driveway, too red to be more than a few hours old, told a different story.

By rights he needed to phone his boss and report what he knew, but it was too early to make that call and what would he say anyway? Hey boss, you know that guy who makes sure we all get a turkey at Christmas and who plays golf with the chief? Well, he might just be a dirty crime lord responsible for murder, arson, and more.

Heck no. Bervoets wasn't telling anyone anything. Not yet. He was going to head back to Antwerp and once he got there he was going to track down Albert Smith and find out just what the old English sleuth knew.

Chapter 36

Franka was forced to wait, a use of her time she was neither familiar with or happy about. Thierry Belvaux worked in the back area of the Laakdal police station, a place where she could not access. Her request to speak with him was acknowledged and the person she talked to, a man with a deeper than usual voice, claimed he passed her message about Dirk De Graaf verbatim.

Yet half an hour passed and she was still sitting on the uncomfortable plastic chair with Endal snoozing at her feet. Patience had never been one of her virtues and she had to fight to stop herself from asking what was taking so long. For all she knew Thierry was busy dealing with criminals. He could be processing a drug dealer or a rapist and she genuinely didn't know how long such a task took.

Another ten minutes ticked by and just when she could feel herself getting ready to complain a door opened to her left and a man came through it.

"I'm looking for Franka Schweiger?" he said.

Franka could tell she was the only person in reception, so his question was an odd one to ask, yet she rose to her feet without making comment.

"Thank you for seeing me," she turned to face the direction of his voice. "I'm speaking to Theirry Belvaux, yes?"

"In the flesh, love."

Franka hated pet names. Always had, but she swallowed it down and offered a smile.

"You remember Dirk De Graaf?" she ended her question on an up cadence, her voice betraying the hope she felt that her trip to Laakdal might bear some fruit.

Thierry took her offered hand and shook it, his hand massive and pudgy in hers. She didn't need to see him to know he was overweight.

"Well, honestly, I would have to focus hard to remember his face and probably wouldn't be able to pick him out of a crowd now. It's been forty years since I last saw him."

Endal gave the man a sniff. Her training included being able to recognise a police officer by their uniform. They were a safe haven if ever she needed help for her human. He smelled of sugar and coffee and she found crystals on his trousers where the donut he'd recently eaten left its mark. She thought about licking the sprinkles up, but resisted.

Shall we sit?" Franka aimed a hand at the chairs. Picking up on Theirry's comment about the length of time since he last saw Dirk, Franka's brain created more and more questions and she needed a moment to run her thoughts through her head.

When Thierry perched, the chair creaking slightly under his weight, Franka followed suit.

"You said 'forty years', has it really been that long since you saw him? You would have been in your early twenties then."

"That's about right."

"You didn't see him when he came back for the funerals?"

Thierry's brow knitted with misunderstanding until he deciphered what Franka meant.

"Oh, you mean his parents' funeral?"

"And his sister's, surely."

"That too," Theirry agreed absentmindedly. "I didn't attend them myself, but I can tell you Dirk didn't either. It was a subject people talked about for a while afterward. To my knowledge the brother-in-law paid for everything and couldn't even get Dirk on the phone. He didn't even send flowers."

Franka reeled from the new information. It was one thing to be a ruthless businessman; she met plenty of those in her work, but to not care that his family were dead? He didn't even send flowers? What did that mean?

It was just a few months after the events of 9/11, so was it PTSD? Could he just not face coming home?

When a stray thought occurred to her, she asked, "Have you ever heard the name 'Kurt Berger'?"

Thierry took a moment to think, but shook his head slowly from side to side, certain he did not. Realising she couldn't see his response, he added, "No, sorry. Should I know who that is?"

It had been a long shot, but it was born of a worrying thought about her father. What if he hadn't been confused about the identity of the man he met in the street? What if his brain had been as clear and dazzlingly brilliant that day as it always used to be? What if Dirk De Graaf was Kurt Berger?

The jump from one idea to the next caught her by surprise because it made sense of everything else. Kurt Berger died in 9/11 but what if he hadn't? If he took the identity of another man and had lived a lie ever since, being identified in the street by an old acquaintance would spark a need to protect his secret.

It was a big leap, but it also explained why her father was attacked and why they came back for a second shot at him in the hospital. The possibility that she could be right made Franka's head spin. She needed to tell Albert, but first she wanted some kind of proof.

Gathering her thoughts and telling her heart to slow down – it was beating so fast – she drew in a calming breath.

"Do you have any pictures of Dirk when he was younger?"

Chapter 37

F inding himself in the elevator, Rex was forced to admit he didn't know what he was supposed to do. He'd been in plenty of elevators before but always had Albert with him. There were buttons above his head and Rex knew he had to do something with them in order to make the magic happen.

Jumping up onto his back legs, he inspected the panel of buttons. They were marked with squiggly lines. Should he press one or all of them? What did the squiggly lines mean?

The doors swished shut before he could touch them.

Rex dropped back down to the floor, guessing he was wrong. It began to move, called from a different floor and when the doors opened again, Rex was surprised and elated to find himself looking out into the lobby. He could smell the drinks in the bar, the potpourri on the reception desk, and the damp city air coming in from the street outside.

The couple waiting to get in jumped when the German Shepherd bounded between them and the staff behind the reception desk shot each other quizzical looks: were they supposed to do something about the dog?

Rex ignored them all. His human was out in the city somewhere and the killers were in their room. The danger had not passed, and he needed to find Albert before anyone else could.

Disappointingly, Rex had no idea where his human could be. He sniffed the air speculatively, hoping he might catch a trace of the old man's scent. It came loaded with a million different odours, but his human was not among them.

He moved away from the hotel. There were people inside watching him and talking; the hotel staff still debating where the dog had come from and what they ought to do about it. Trotting along the street, Rex caught a mark that he'd left the previous evening – he walked back this way from Endal's house.

Presented with a direction he could go and a destination at the end where he could expect to find humans he knew, humans who might be able to locate Albert, Rex set off. It was a way to go, but he had no better option to pursue and believed he'd left enough markers to lead him all the way there without getting lost.

Chapter 38

The final straw came just before lunch. His secret had always been vulnerable from two directions: America where it was possible someone would question the authenticity of Kurt Berger's remains, and from Dirk De Graaf's hometown an hour's drive from his current location.

Many times he had questioned his decision to set up in Antwerp so close to where Dirk grew up, but the passport he took from Dirk's Manhattan apartment that day was soon to expire and at the time he didn't have the contacts to obtain a fake one so easily. Belgium was his obvious destination and though he planned to organise himself and move on, it took him almost no time at all to score his first deal. That led to the next and before he knew it he'd been in Antwerp for three months.

The worry he felt over someone from Dirk's life discovering his false identity diminished greatly once he had identified and killed the man's family.

That Dirk had to die was unfortunate, he genuinely liked him, but Kurt knew there had been no other option. It only took until noon on Dirk's first day at Bryant Investments for someone to identify how closely the two men resembled each other. They often joked about it, but it wasn't as though they were twins. Dirk was an inch taller and had a lot more body hair. He admitted he was likely to go bald as he aged; all the men in his family lost their hair in their late thirties and forties.

Dirk's eyes were a different colour too, a deep green where Kurt's were blue, but the shape of their faces, noses, chins, and smiles were very similar. Similar enough that Kurt seized upon a chance when God presented it. Not that he believed in God. Kurt believed the strong survive and that the ruthless will always beat the strong.

The FBI were breathing down his neck. He'd managed to bury his activities behind a bunch of false firms and paperwork, but when he got a call from one of the people he'd employed and subsequently aided financially along the way, he knew his time was short.

That day was September 11th.

Dirk was hurt when the plane struck the north tower. The ceiling came down and though it was made of flimsy panels to cover the ductwork and electrics above he was bleeding profusely from a cut to his scalp and struggling to see.

Half the people in the office ran out the door like they were in an Olympic sprint event. The rest followed, everyone thinking just one thought: get out. Dirk wasn't the only one injured, but he was the worst and Kurt almost left him behind. Almost. No one knew at the time that a plane had hit the building or that it was a terrorist attack, but his sense of self-preservation kicked in instantly and he would have been first out the door had his desk not been one of the furthest from the exit.

Dirk called for help and in that moment, Kurt could see his escape route. Not just from the building, but from his whole life. He was growing bored with his wife. She was beautiful with an amazing body, but being shackled to one woman didn't suit him, not at that age. Worse than that was the child. He foolishly agreed to her desire to have kids, but the damned thing never slept. At two years old, she had never once let him have a full night's sleep and he resented her for it.

How was he supposed to operate and succeed in such circumstances?

Some of the windows had blown out from the devastating impact of the plane, so when Kurt heard a scream and saw a body fall past his floor, he pushed Dirk out through one. He was already unconscious and bleeding to death from his injuries – the ones Kurt inflicted. To ensure Dirk would be identified as Kurt Berger, Kurt knocked him out with a four-hole punch. He swapped their suits and placed his wallet and watch on his former friend. Only at the last minute did he think about fingerprints.

He started on the right hand, bludgeoning the digits until there was too little left for anyone to piece together a print. He was about to start on the left when he remembered Dirk's tattoo. If ever there was a mark that would identify the body, that was it.

An office guillotine helped to take care of that. It was designed for cutting through sheets of paper, but broken apart the blade could be swung with enough effort to do the job. He rolled Dirk's shirt and jacket sleeves up to do the job, and pulled them back down afterward.

With the false trail set, all he needed to do was leave. Dirk's house keys were in a bag next to his desk along with his stinky gym kit from that morning's workout. Kurt put the sweaty clothes on without a second thought.

He was Dirk De Graaf now.

He could learn to speak French, or whatever language they favoured in Belgium, and work on his accent over the next few weeks, but he was leaving America on the first flight out. It didn't matter where he went just so long as he never came back.

Kurt/Dirk reflected on the memory now, how on edge he'd felt for months. He felt the same level of stress now, though it was different because back then it was only his paranoia making him jump at shadows, now he knew they were on to him, and that he had a limited window in which he could up and disappear again.

The notification from the surveillance team in New York was bad enough, but the call from Laakdal proved to be the final straw. It was another safety measure he'd put in place. He'd killed Dirk's parents and sister; certain they would learn he was back in the country and would choose to visit. He could ignore them, but that only increased the likelihood they would show up unannounced. There were also friends Dirk grew up with, but how was Kurt supposed to know which ones? Old school records showed who was in his class, but that wasn't the same thing.

Regardless, he couldn't kill everyone.

As a compromise, he found a few people he could payoff to keep their ears and eyes open. He didn't do it himself; he didn't dare set foot in Laakdal, but money can buy you anything.

He received one call from a woman at the post office and another from the police station. Franka Schweiger, Erich Jannings' daughter, was in Dirk's hometown asking questions. It was the final nail in the coffin, but in many ways he was glad of it.

Until the calls came he'd spent the day debating whether his decision to run was the right one. There were gaps but he could plug them. Kill Erich, kill the annoying Englishman, kill anyone else who got in his way, but now he had the double whammy. People in America knew, and Franka Schweiger was stirring up trouble in Laakdal. It was an hour from Antwerp and far too close for comfort.

There were a few last things to do; a clean sweep was required to leave behind as little evidence as possible, but one way or another he was leaving today and there would be a body left behind the police would identify as his.

Chapter 39

F or the first time in a long time, Franka was angry about the limitations her blindness imposed. She rarely gave it a second thought; things were how they were. Right now though a set of eyes would help.

Thierry couldn't leave work, but was generous enough to make a phone call to his wife. There were some old photograph albums in his attic where he believed there existed a few pages of shots from one summer when he was much younger. Dirk appeared in those pictures and Franka could have them provided his wife, Emily, could find them.

Endal walked her back to the car and Josse drove them to the address Thierry gave her. Emily knew to expect a visitor and met Franka at the door.

"I managed to find them," she revealed, leading Franka into her house. "They were nowhere near where Thierry said they were, but that's so typical of men, don't you think?"

Franka mumbled a reply, not wanting to point out that her husband was systematic about putting everything exactly back in the spot it was supposed to inhabit otherwise she wouldn't be able to find it.

Endal sniffed the air. A cat lived in the house. It was middle-aged and probably getting saggy around its core for she could also smell mouse droppings.

The woman who lived in the house – her scent was everywhere as was that of the police officer they had just been talking to – led them into the living room where she invited Franka to sit.

Endal led her to the couch, making sure to connect her with it so she could feel the arm and know where to sit.

"I took a couple of pictures with my phone, just to have Thierry confirm I was looking at the right person. I guess you can't see what I am holding, but I have half a dozen shots of a man my husband assures me is Dirk De Graaf. I guess he would know because they have the same tattoo."

"Tattoo?"

"Yeah. Thierry told me he got it in Amsterdam on a drunken weekend with a couple of his mates. He might have told me their names, but I must not have committed them to memory. They got them on their left forearms."

"What does it look like?"

Emily pulled a face before responding, questioning what descriptive terms she could use to explain to a blind person what anything looked like. Should she mention colours? Would a blind person know what blue looked like?

Pushing on regardless, she said, "The tattoo is of a man smoking a large joint. I guess that's what they got up to in Amsterdam. Thierry wasn't a police officer back then."

Franka's phone cut through the quiet afternoon stillness, ringing loudly from inside her handbag. The voice software announced, "Unknown number calling," and proceeded to recite the number.

Franka found the right button and answered before it was halfway through.

"Franka Schweiger. How may I help you?" She expected it to be a client or a prospective client; her card got given out just like anyone else's.

"Mrs Schweiger, this is former FBI agent Margaret Bloomfield. I need a few minutes of your time to discuss a man called Kurt Berger."

"He faked his death, didn't he?" The words slipped from her mouth without consulting her brain, a terrible thing for a lawyer to do, yet she regretted her rash question not one bit because she knew she was right. She had been thinking it since speaking with Thierry and though she was yet to voice it, the call from an FBI agent, former or otherwise, was enough to drive home a dagger of certainty.

The response caught Margaret off guard. She expected to have to explain who Kurt Berger was and how it came to be that Franka heard the name.

Blinking her surprise away, she said, "Yes, I believe he did. Do you know what alias he is using?"

Chapter 40

Lieutenant Bervoets hunched over his screen. He'd broken the speed limit most of the way back to Antwerp, employing his lights and sirens when he needed to move traffic out of his way. Throughout the whole journey he argued with himself. Clues were pointing at one of the city's richest businessmen, but they were all circumstantial and easy to ignore.

Until one pushed them all together.

A dead P.I. who was looking into Dirk De Graaf is tortured and killed. A lawyer reports that her elderly father got into a heated confrontation with the same man just a day earlier and it is then claimed that the men Bervoets believed to be opportunistic muggers came back for a second go at killing the elderly man while he was still in a coma in hospital.

He had no proof the altercation ever took place and there was nothing other than the word of Albert Smith to suggest the same muggers returned. If he told his boss he would be laughed out of his office, but every fibre of Bervoets' being screamed at him to pay attention.

According to Harold De Waele's assistant, the murdered P.I. didn't have any other ongoing cases other than a couple of divorce assists where he was expected to catch a spouse in bed with someone who was not their partner. It meant it had to be the De Graaf investigation that got him killed. Combine with that the conveniently burned-out office and the disappearance of the clients who hired De Waele to look into De Graaf and it all suddenly became quite damning.

At the same time it was nothing.

There was no actual evidence to link Dirk De Graaf to anything.

Using the Erich Jannings case, which was still live, Bervoets began to nose around. Where had De Graaf come from? Who was he? What connection did he have to the Poelvoordes?

Their business was third generation, a technology firm with a large factory located on the north bank of the river. Bervoets guessed they hadn't moved fast enough when technology changed – it happened to big firms so there was no reason why it couldn't happen to the little guy. However, when he researched their firm he realised he knew the name. They were not so little. Another search showed their annual statements. They had been doing exceptionally well, recording sales in excess of ten million Euros many years in a row. However, that was before Patrick Poelvoorde, the founder's grandson, took over.

The reports told him nothing of what befell the company and he wasn't financially savvy enough to read between the lines. However, the dwindling profits and sudden losses were easy to spot. They gambled, lost, gambled bigger and lost even worse.

Quite how De Graaf fitted into that Bervoets didn't yet know, but delving deeper, he committed to finding out.

Chapter 41

A lbert was just arriving back at the hotel when his phone began to ring. The number was unknown, but for all he knew it was the hotel calling to say Rex had given some poor housekeeping woman a heart attack.

"Albert Smith."

"Mr Smith, my name is Margaret Bloomfield. I've just been speaking to Franka Schweiger about Kurt Berger."

It was an introduction that grabbed his attention. So too the American accent. He couldn't place which state it might hail from, but he was all ears to hear what she had to say.

Standing in front of the hotel where his conversation at least seemed more private than it would in the lobby, Albert nodded along to the information Margaret had to share. Every bit of it made sense, not only of the current situation, but of Erich's confusion, which, it turned out, was nothing of the sort.

"Franka sent me some photographs of Dirk De Graaf," Margaret explained. "The pictures are a quarter of a century old and the quality isn't great, but he's the spitting image of Kurt Berger at the same age. Also, Dirk had a tattoo on his left forearm and the body identified as Kurt's was missing below the elbow. That's hardly conclusive, but I believe the man Erich Jannings met is the real Kurt Berger. He pulled a vanishing trick to escape justice and has been living here as Dirk De Graaf ever since."

Albert took it all in. His police career could be measured in decades, but he'd never come across a case like this one. Margaret outlined the investigation in 2001. It hinted at a man who was prepared to do anything to get an edge over his competition. By Albert's estimation, Kurt/Dirk had figured a few things out along the way so that when he set up again in a new country with a new identity, he kept enough distance between his visible business and the illegal activities underpinning it for no one to ever look his way.

He'd created an empire upon which he perched as a very rich man.

Margaret was on her way to Antwerp, calling him from her car using the number Franka provided. She was twenty minutes out and wanted to know where they could meet.

He gave the address for his hotel and let the call end. Rex was inside and though he felt quite certain his dog had done nothing but sleep all morning, it was time they were back together. With a little time to kill he could take him for a walk and be ready for Margaret's arrival.

It felt good to have someone else on his side and his mood was close to buoyant as he rode the elevator up through the hotel. It changed the instant he got to his room.

Rex wasn't there and his room had been tossed. The contents of his suitcase and backpack were strewn across the floor, but it was the blood that worried him the most. Unlike his dog, he couldn't tell the red stains on the hotel's white sheets were from a human, not from Rex, and fear gripped his heart.

The blood extended into the ensuite bathroom where someone had dripped it all over the sink and the tile beneath before doing a shoddy job of cleaning it up.

The attempt to clean the mess told Albert it probably wasn't Rex's blood, but he also knew he was being optimistic. He needed to question the hotel staff. They would have CCTV cameras in the lobby, but whether they had picked up Rex being led or carried from the building, or if the people who took him even came in that way sounded doubtful.

Gritting his teeth, his mind a whirl with anguishing thoughts, Albert snatched at his phone when it rang. Franka's name was on the screen, but his intention to tell her Rex was missing died in his throat when she delivered her terrible news first.

Chapter 42

When he reached the hotel lobby, Albert ran from the elevator to get to the hotel's front desk. There was a woman in her fifties with a Pomeranian in her arms complaining about something insignificant, and with no time to wait Albert all but shoved her out of the way.

"My room has been broken into!" he snapped at volume to get the attention of the concierge staff. "It's trashed, there is blood all over the place, and my dog is missing."

"Do you mind?" demanded the woman with the Pomeranian.

Albert spared her a glance. "No, I don't." While she huffed and complained, he blurted, "Call the police and don't let anyone into my room. The blood is forensic evidence." He was already moving toward the door when he had a better idea. "In fact, call Lieutenant Bervoets. Can you write that down? Bervoets." He spelled it out. "Tell him Albert Smith's room has been tossed and his dog is missing." Message delivered, he ran out through the hotel doors, missing the reception staff calling after him - they had seen his dog leaving of its own accord.

He flagged down a passing taxi and yelled an instruction the moment he yanked the door open. He had to get to Universitair Ziekenhuis Hospital as fast as possible. Franka had just received a call from their administration to say her father's security detail had been found.

They were both dead.

In the back of the car he chewed his nails. He wanted to be out looking for Rex. The dog was bright enough to stay close to the hotel, at least Albert hoped he was, but even as he thought that he remembered the times Rex had chosen to set off on his own. It was as though the dog had his own missions to complete.

Erich had to come first, not because he was human or more important – he wasn't more important to Albert – but because Albert acknowledged how little there was that he could do to find Rex. Of course, in all likelihood there would also be nothing he could do about Erich. If his security guards were dead, so was he.

Or he'd been taken, but if the latter were true, it could only be so they could kill him elsewhere.

Franka had been in a state, crying down the phone and begging Albert to help. There was no way to refuse her request. She could have asked her husband, but he worked outside of the city, so Albert was closest by a long way.

His leg twitched with impatience until he forced it to stop. His heart was racing from the adrenalin and anxiety. He wanted to be doing something positive, something that would help, but they were behind from the start and just didn't get enough time to catch up.

Knowing who was behind it all might mean they got to beat him in the end, but at what cost? What if Rex was already dead? He couldn't think it without a lump forming in his throat. He would get them. He would get Dirk De Graaf or Kurt Berger or whatever his real name might be.

Albert's hand reached for his phone, hesitating and returning to his lap where he clasped it with the other. He'd thought about calling Bervoets. Not that he had the lieutenant's number, but a call to the police would find its way to him soon enough. He stopped only because he couldn't be sure what the detective would do. He could help at the hospital, but they would have called the police before they phoned Franka so someone at the station already knew about Erich Jannings.

His greater concern was Bervoets' general attitude. His last words were a promise to lock him up and charge him if he caught Albert continuing to investigate. That he had been right all along would not necessarily make a difference straight away. Furthermore, the worry that he could be on Kurt Berger's payroll continued. Albert thought it unlikely – his actions were the result of blindness and stupidity, yet it could not be ruled out, so when the taxi ditched him at the kerb in front of the hospital, Albert accepted that he was alone and staying that way.

The plaza leading to the main entrance was filled with people coming and going again. Some of them patients stepping outside to get some air, identifiable by their bedclothes or sportswear and slippers. The majority though were dressed for the cold, December air. Albert had to duck and weave between them. Mumbled words of apology following his passage as he forged through the doors.

He'd left less than forty minutes earlier and was back already, his day turning to one where he was in perpetual motion and achieving next to nothing.

There were no police in sight, but he found them soon enough when he got to Erich's room. Not that he got to Erich's room, he was stopped ten yards shy by a young man in uniform.

"I'm sorry, Sir, there's been an incident."

"I know. That's what I am here for. I just need to know, was Erich Jannings taken or did they kill him in his bed?"

Chapter 43

The news about her father, or more accurately, her father's security sent Franka into a panicked flight back to Antwerp. She left Emily's home in tears, convinced De Graaf's thugs had finally got to him.

The deputy head of hospital security was on her phone even as she had Endal race her to the car. It was an emerging situation, and they were, at that time, unclear what had happened. Her father was missing and both members of the security team she hired had been found dead inside his room.

They were searching the hospital and had teams on every exit to check anyone attempting to leave with an unconscious patient. The deputy sounded confident, but expressed how limited their manpower was. Security at the hospital was there to deal with emergencies not to act as a policing force or to apprehend criminals.

Franka begged him to find her father, but she held out little hope they would or that he would be alive if they did. He was old and becoming ever increasingly confused by the world around him and she knew her time with him was now limited. None of that mattered though because he was her dad and he deserved to die at home in comfort in his own bed.

She kept the man on the line longer than was necessary, hoping an update would come while they were talking. It didn't and she was forced to let him go after keeping him tied up for more than ten minutes.

By then Josse was speeding them back to Antwerp on the E313, breaking the limit on Franka's command. It was only once she was off the phone that she had thought to call Albert. He responded as she knew he would; by reassuring her he was on his way and would report once he got there.

He needed time to get back to the hospital though and for the next half an hour all Franka could do was fret and wish her phone would ring. She felt sick and she wanted to cry, but the tears had dried after the initial shock and now refused to flow. They would return when the news was confirmed, but while she so keenly wanted someone to call her, the longer it took them the better the news had to be, right?

"Is that her car?" asked Billal, checking with his brother not because he doubted his ability to identify a make and model, but to make sure Medhi had seen it too and was ready.

They were parked down the street from her house where they had been waiting for more than an hour. It had been a busy morning; they were getting all the work now that Jonas and Matthias had vanished. They'd never had any respect for the local thugs and their recent incompetence upheld their opinion.

They expected De Graaf to demand they find and kill the two idiots, but that order was yet to come and they were tied up with other tasks such as fetching the blind woman.

Endal lifted her head when the car cruised to a stop, the familiar crunch of the gravel on the driveway confirming they were home as much as the suburb's familiar smells. She liked the car, especially when they took longer journeys. She could snooze contentedly stretched out on the backseat with her head on Franka's lap. She would put an arm around her head and idly scratch at the fur on her shoulder for comfort.

Easing herself off the leather to sit up, she looked out through the front screen to their house beyond. Everything appeared as it should. Except …

She caught the unfamiliar scent of the two men when Josse opened the driver's door to get out. There was nothing about their smell to cause alarm apart from its close proximity and the edge of fear it contained.

Triggered by recent events, Endal came to a guard stance in time to see the men she could smell running toward Josse. Franka's driver never stood a chance and barely saw them coming until it was too late to defend himself.

Billal jabbed the stun gun into his neck, watched for the half second it took for Josse's eyes to roll upward and turned his attention to the real target.

Endal darted through the gap between the seats, clambering awkwardly into the front only to find her way barred when Billal kicked the door shut in her face.

Taking the impact to her nose and lucky to have not caught one of her front paws in the closing gap, Endal recoiled. She wanted to take a second, but a cry of alarm from Franka made her shake off the pain in her face.

Medhi had one knee on the back seat and a grip on Franka. He sliced through her seatbelt with a razor-sharp blade and stunned her with his own gun.

Fear drew a bark from Endal's lips and she flew through the gap once more, moving as fast as she could to save her human. Too late though, Medhi wrenched Franka's deadweight from the car and kicked the door shut.

This time Endal wasn't close enough for it to hurt her, but threw herself at the unyielding barrier in her desperation to get through it. Again and again she charged the glass, ramming it with her skull and barking all the while.

Franka hung limply over Medhi's shoulder, her arms and legs dangling and swaying in rhythm with his stride.

Endal continued to go nuts, unable to fully comprehend what she was seeing and as she stared, her front paws on the leather of the door, the window started to move. It came down an inch, stopping when it startled Endal and caused her to move.

The fresh air spilling from outside carried the scent of the two men, a scent she would never forget. Her body quivered with the need to get out and stop them, but she forced herself to calm. The window had started to open, but what had she done to make it do that?

Placing her paws back on the window ledge, she waited and watched but nothing happened.

Billal was already at the car, moving faster without the burden of a human to carry. He popped the boot, swinging it high and wide open then jogged to the driver's door and had the car started before his brother was able to dump Franka into the car's rear end.

Endal focused on the door and the window, trying to remember where her paws had been when the window started to move. She shifted her right front paw and felt something shift beneath one claw.

The window sprang to life with an almost silent buzz, descending into the door.

Endal shoved her head through the gap, driving off with her back legs only to find the gap was still too small. Yanking her skull back inside, she found the button once more and this time waited the extra second to be sure she had a gap wide enough for her bulky frame.

She hit the ground running, her legs threatening to burst into flames if they went any faster.

Medhi was at the passenger's door and about to slide in when he caught the dog's movement from the corner of his eye. He'd been moving swiftly already, now was not the time to hang around, but the incoming rage-hound propelled him inside the car with a shout.

Billal took off like he had the devil on his tail, mashing the accelerator so convincingly the wheels spun in place for a half second before finding purchase. The car leapt forward, fishtailing away from the kerb with both men hanging on tight.

Ten yards later and in the middle of the road, Billal checked the rear-view mirror and was shocked to see not one dog in pursuit but two.

It took Rex more than an hour to find his way back to Endal's house, first following his own scent and as he drew closer, detecting Endal's. That led him right to his intended destination, but before he could get there he saw Billal and Medhi. Rex didn't know their names, but he remembered them handling his human and he knew their presence so close to Endal's house could not be a good thing.

By the time the breeze delivered their scents, confirming what he already knew, Rex was running at his fastest pace. He couldn't keep it up for long, but he sure covered a lot of ground quickly. Not quickly enough to stop the attack though.

Rex heard Endal bark and the car door slam. He heard Endal cry out in pain and saw when one of the men dragged Franka from the car. He was still a hundred yards away and already moving as fast as his legs could carry him.

He pushed on, his lungs beginning to sear from the effort of his full sprint, and was relieved to see Endal appear ahead of him. She looked to be unhurt and was giving chase just as Rex was. They weren't going to catch the car though. Not once it was moving.

Rex accepted his limitations with a frustrated bark.

Jerking her head to the side when she heard Rex bark, Endal saw the swifter dog draw level.

"They took my human!" Endal barked her fear and anger.

Rex had no breath left to reply and he knew that pushing hard for much longer was not an option - his legs were starting to shake from the effort.

The car powered on, leaving the dogs in a cloud of exhaust gas left in its wake.

Endal cried out, "No!"

Panting hard, Rex stopped to get his breath and managed to say, "Don't worry, we'll find her."

Chapter 44

For Albert the news that Erich had been found alive, well, and even conscious, was every bit as shocking as the news of the most recent attempt on his life. By calculation he'd awoken not long after Albert's attempts to revive him. It prompted the security guard standing watch at that time to alert the medical staff.

They came to his room, but when they removed the intubation tube from his throat, Erich began to choke uncontrollably and relapsed into unconsciousness. The doctor briefing Albert reported that his irregular heartrate and dropping blood pressure appeared to be a (some long-winded medical term Albert couldn't understand) and they rushed him back to surgery.

Mercifully, surgery proved unnecessary, Erich's vitals stabilising even as they prepped him to go back under the knife. However, while he was in their care, someone attacked the security guards, the two men left temporarily unemployed while their principal was in an area they couldn't enter.

Their bodies were found in the hospital room's private bathroom by a nurse, but the resulting panic and search for the missing patient were unknown to the team looking after Erich. It was a catalogue of small events that led to the confusion.

The good news was that Erich survived yet another attack on his life. He was awake again and being closely monitored. It was great news, and just as pleasing was the sudden glut of police officers. A double homicide on hospital grounds gave credence to Albert's claim that Erich Jannings was in danger. His private security team might be gone, but he was protected better than ever now.

Albert asked to see him and was granted permission, but wanted to let Franka know first.

His brow furrowed when she failed to answer. He tried her number again and again, each time waiting until it rang off. Quelling a rising worry, he sent her a text message, confirming her father was unharmed and that he was with him.

The police were everywhere he looked, quizzing hospital staff, interviewing the sobbing nurse who found the bodies, viewing the security footage from around the hospital as they tried to find anything that might identify the killer or killers, and most likely queuing up to get answers from Erich himself.

He found a chair and slumped into it. If Erich was awake and the police were interviewing him the case was over. Franka wanted him to figure out who attacked her father and why. Erich would be able to tell them most of that and from his brief conversation with Margaret Bloomfield, the retired FBI agent, he was confident the circle around Dirk De Graaf/Kurt Berger was closing in fast.

How could it not?

Under any other circumstances, it would be time for Albert to relax, to put his feet up, to have a pint perhaps, or maybe even just pack his bags and move on. He couldn't do any of those things though because Rex was missing.

His priority switched from solving the mystery and saving Erich to finding his dog. Nothing else mattered. The police might help, but they were already busy and had a big arrest to make in the not-too-distant future.

Telling himself Rex would be easy to find and that he probably hadn't strayed too far from the hotel, Albert pushed down on his knees to get back to his feet. That was when it hit him: Rex had a tracking chip!

Giddy from a sudden sense of euphoria, he yanked his phone from an inside coat pocket and scrolled to find the App. He'd never used it, hoping he would never have to, and possessed only a rudimentary understanding of how it worked.

However, when it opened, filling his screen with a map of the city, it showed two points highlighted with 3D pins. One was him and the other was Rex. It looked as though Rex's pin was moving. All he had to do was navigate his way to him.

He was yet to speak with Erich, but knew it could wait. Franka's father was safe, and the police were now involved – he could walk away and feel confident everything would work out just fine.

Hurrying to the hospital's main entrance, he left through the automatic doors and angled left. There was a tram stop dead ahead, but to find Rex he needed something that could go wherever he pointed and that demanded yet another taxi.

He cut through the plaza, making his way past the people coming and going, and turning left when he rounded the trees. He dipped his head at a couple of paramedics looking his way, his mind too full of thoughts of Rex to notice they fell into step behind him.

There were taxis ahead, a short line of them with the drivers keeping warm inside. They might have been there for minutes or hours for all Albert knew but he was certain the cab at the front would be pleased to get a passenger.

The hard nose of a gun in his right kidney caught him by complete surprise. A hand gripped his left bicep in a vicelike grip and a voice growled in his ear, "Make a sound and I shoot you right here."

Chapter 45

They knew they were in trouble. They had known it for some time because they were savvy enough to read the signs. They were the B-team to Billal and Medhi, but those two thought they were too good for their boss to manage without. It never seemed to occur to the Iranian brothers why there had been a job opening for them.

Dirk De Graaf was the most cunning and most dangerous man they had ever worked for. They knew almost nothing about him because he shared nothing. They were given jobs to do and they carried them out. Sometimes they pleased him and got a bonus, other times the job they were sent to complete didn't go according to plan and they collectively questioned if he might just have them killed.

That was what happened to the men Billal and Medhi replaced. At least, that's what Jonas and Matthias believed. The previous pair were just gone one day. They had messed up, that much they knew, failing to kill a minor politician who stood in the way of a deal their boss was trying to broker. It cost him millions and a few days later the other team were nowhere to be found and the Iranian brothers were in their place.

Jonas and Matthias hadn't cost their boss any money that they knew of, but they had never seen him so on edge either. He wanted an old man mugged and killed – no problem. Except a problem was precisely what it turned out to be. The Englishman with his dog showed up and ruined their perfectly executed plan. He did the same thing when they tried again and had continued to defeat their best efforts to take him out of the picture too.

They tracked Albert Smith to his hiding place at a plush hotel where they ought have been able to kill his dog and wait in hiding until he returned but that backfired when the crazy German Shepherd came at them before they could even get through the door.

Since the first mistake their every effort had been to undo the error and make it good. In a final roll of the dice, final because they were giving serious consideration to skipping town and never coming back, they stole paramedics' uniforms and had one last go at killing Erich Jannings. The disguises allowed them to sneak up on the security guards and they burst through the door triumphantly – Ha! Take that Billal and Mehdi and your stupid stun guns!

How could they have known their target wasn't in his room?

Defeated again, they had been on their way out of the hospital when they spotted none other than Albert Smith on his way in. It was a consolation prize, but far better than nothing at all. If they waited for him to exit, they could take him to De Graaf and maybe redeem themselves enough to stay in his employment. There were no other gigs that paid as well.

Leering at the old man, they manoeuvred him into a maintenance area at the side of the hospital. They were out of sight and dressed as paramedics, so no one would question them carrying an unconscious man. Or even a bleeding man; Matthias grinned at the thought.

They weren't going to knock him out just yet though. If they had him, maybe they could still get Jannings, and that would change everything.

"Erich Jannings," Matthias demanded, jabbing Albert in the gut with his gun. "Where is he?"

Albert's initial burst of shock and fear was subsiding. He was faced with a pair of thugs, but if they were going to simply kill him, they would have done so already.

"You're hurt," he observed, looking at the smaller man. His face thoughtful, he guessed, "Rex got you, didn't he?" It brought a smile to his face which Matthias removed with another painful jab to Albert's ribs.

Albert doubled over but kept his eyes on their faces, watching in case they jubilantly claimed to have hurt his dog worse than he hurt them. It would have come instantly had that been the case so when a second passed and they hadn't replied, he gave his dog a mental congratulations and allowed a sense of relief to wash over him.

"Let's just kill him here and be done with it," Jonas growled. "We can send De Graaf pictures."

"Oh, I wouldn't do that," said a voice from behind them.

Albert ducked to the side to look around Matthias' bulk and both thugs turned their head to see, their guns training onto the retirement-age woman standing a few yards away.

She was American and her confidence in such a situation was good enough confirmation for Albert to believe he was meeting Margaret Bloomfield. He could have picked better circumstances to make a new acquaintance, like perhaps running away from an exploding volcano. Their odds might be better, but if the guns posed a threat, she seemed not to notice.

"Hello." She smiled at Jonas and Matthias, raised her right hand and made it look like a gun. With her index finger pointing upwards, she said, "If either one of you so much as twitches in a way I don't like, I will give the sniper permission to fire. All I have to do is point."

Jonas and Matthias turned their heads inward to look at each other whereupon Jonas' eyes doubled in size and he pointed to his colleague's chest where a small red dot sat an inch from his heart.

Fearing the same was true of him, Jonas dropped his gun and ran, hands wrapped around his head as though they would do anything to protect against a high velocity bullet. Matthias had not the first clue who the new player was, but seeing his partner flee was enough to make him copy.

His weapon hit the ground in his wake as he ran terrified past the woman and vanished around the corner.

Albert's jaw hung open and his eyes searched the rooftops opposite while he forced his body back to fully upright and rubbed at his bruised gut.

Margaret sagged, a sigh of great relief escaping her body with an accompanying chuckle.

"I never for a second thought that would actually work."

About to ask what she meant, Albert's stunned eyes watch her pick a laser pointer off the wall to her right. It was attached to a bunch of keys. There was no sniper, it was just her and the ballsiest bluff he'd ever seen.

"Margaret?" he sought to confirm, still blown away by her bravery.

She dropped the keys and laser pointer into her handbag, "And you must be Albert Smith." She came forward, right hand extended.

"How did you find me?" Albert did nothing to hide the disbelief in his voice.

"Ah," she stooped to collect first one gun and then the other, placing both in her handbag. "I tracked your phone."

"You can do that?" Albert felt like he was talking to James Bond's better trained, more capable, female equivalent.

He got a grin in reply. "Who were those two, anyway? Something to do with Kurt Berger?" She had aimed her feet back toward the path and with no reason to hang around in the maintenance area, Albert followed.

"Probably," Albert replied as honestly as he could. "Almost certainly, I would say, but I don't know for sure. They are the ones who attacked Erich Jannings and they are probably guilty of killing the security guards Franka hired to protect him."

The murders were news to Margaret, and Albert, despite his desire to go in search of Rex, would have filled her in had Lieutenant Bervoets not chosen that precise moment to show up.

Chapter 46

The dogs tracked the exhaust smell for more than a mile before they were no longer able to tell where it had gone. By then Rex's heartrate and breathing had returned to something near normal, aided by the winter air that helped to cool his body.

That was good news. The bad news was they had no clue which direction to go.

Stopping at the edge of the road Endal looked forlorn.

"*They're going to hurt her,*" she whined, sadness overwhelming her. "*She's so helpless without me.*"

"*No, we're going to stop them before they get the chance to do that,*" Rex countered, doing his best to sound confident.

"*How?*" Endal's reply came loaded with the frustration she felt. If they had no scent to follow, they had no way to find Franka.

Rex came to stand in front of her, his eyes calm and determined.

"*What did they smell of?*"

"*What?*"

"*Come on,*" Rex coached. "*Tell me what they smelled of. You must have got a good whiff when they took her. So what did you find that stood out in the background.*"

Endal shrugged. "*What difference does it make? Even if I tell you that they both carried a trace of old oil, burnt steel, and pigeon poop, how does that help us? They had been near water too, but Antwerp has miles of riverfront property so it's not like we can use that to narrow it down.*"

"Maybe not," Rex grinned, *"but I think I know someone who can."* Excited to test out his theory, Rex started walking.

"Where are you going?" Endal called after him, but Rex just called her a slowcoach and told her to catch up. They had a lift to catch.

Two minutes later, standing in line for the next tram as it approached, Endal questioned, *"Remind me again how this will work?"*

"It's too far to walk into town, especially if we then need to go somewhere else, so we take the tram."

"But we don't have a human with us," Endal pointed out confused. Dogs rode human transport with humans. Anything else was just confusing. How would they know when to get off?

"Look at me," Rex insisted. *"What am I doing?"*

"Um, waiting in line for a tram?" Endal hazarded a guess that the answer would be obvious and not cryptic.

"Almost. I am waiting in line for a tram with my human."

"That's not your human," Endal argued.

"But does anyone else know that? If I get on next to him and sit real close by his side, will anyone think to question what I am doing?"

"That's ... genius!" Endal was suitably impressed. *"But hold on. How do we know when to get off?"*

"Ah, that's the easy part."

Chapter 47

"**M**r Smith," he called to make sure Albert had seen him and changed his trajectory to intercept.

"Here to arrest me?" Albert accused, reminding the senior detective of their previous encounters and his most recent promise.

Bervoets held up his hands in surrender. "No, Mr Smith, I think we can put what has gone before behind us now. I fear you may be right about Dirk De Graaf." Lieutenant Bervoets was yet to find anything to incriminate the rich stockbroker, but he had called in a favour with two men from the financial crimes division. They were going to take a close look at De Graaf's business activities starting with his connection to the Poelvoordes' bankrupt firm. If there was something to find, they would uncover it.

Recognising a fellow law enforcement officer, Margaret stepped forward to shake his hand.

"I believe you mean Kurt Berger, not Dirk De Graaf." She gave Bervoets a second to look confused before explaining what she believed she knew. It was a revelation and a half.

The detective asked, "Does he know you are back on his trail?"

Margaret said, "I hope not, but I cannot rule it out. This is one wily operator we are dealing with. I think he killed Dirk De Graaf to steal his identity and Franka Schweiger believes she uncovered something in his hometown of Laakdal. He may have killed Dirk's parents and sister to limit the likelihood of exposure."

Bervoets wasn't often stunned, but a man he claimed only yesterday could not be in any way involved in anything shady appeared to be at the centre of a series of crimes. If Margaret Bloomfield was right, they went back years and had gone undetected for all that time.

"Where is Mrs Schweiger now?" Bervoets asked, wondering how it was that the American woman was so well informed. How long had she been in Antwerp gathering evidence?

Albert was about to say that Franka wasn't answering her phone when a ringing noise came from his pocket. Thinking he ought to check it before making his announcement, he heard Margaret explain that Franka was on her way back to Antwerp and should be with them soon.

Relieved to see Franka's name on his screen, Albert thumbed the green button and lifted the phone to his ear. He wanted to leave to look for Rex, but the arrival of Lieutenant Bervoets was delaying him. The detective was leading Margaret into the hospital where he planned to speak with Erich Jannings. They had already made it back into the hospital lobby where there was a steady hum of conversation.

He said, "Franka?" and jabbed his right index finger into his other ear to make it easier to hear her reply.

"Mr Smith, I'm afraid Franka cannot come to the phone right now." A chill swept through Albert's body. He had only met Dirk De Graaf one time and they shared very few words, but there was no question in his mind that he was talking to him again now.

Margaret and Lieutenant Bervoets were still walking, their exchange of information taking them farther and farther away from Albert. He could no longer hear what they were saying but he could hear the Dirk/Kurt's voice when it spoke again.

"Listen carefully, Mr Smith. This is what you are going to do."

Chapter 48

K urt Berger placed his phone back into his pocket and nodded to Billal.

"Fetch him."

The brothers set off without need for a verbal response. They were curious about what was happening, but wise enough not to question the boss. He was never forthcoming with answers when they did.

Their departure left Kurt alone with his victims. And victims they were about to be. He just needed one more to join the party and he could get things started. Ruthless efficiency was a term he'd lived by for much of his adult life and it had always done him proud.

Now a little after one in the afternoon, he'd spent the morning making his money disappear. He was going to lose about half of it, but that would still leave him with more than enough to start again. He had thirty plus years to live yet and planned to see them out in comfort. It was a shame that he had to leave his wife behind; he'd enjoyed her company and their intimate moments far more than he had with Andrea, but he knew without asking that she would never understand.

Were he to reveal his true identity to Ingrid, she might accept the truth of it, but he couldn't tell her that he abandoned his first wife and had killed the real Dirk De Graaf. Ingrid would never look at him the same, so he took things for how they were and instead of being upset or disappointed, embraced the excitement that would be his new-found singledom.

A rich bachelor, that was how he would present himself ... No! A widower! Far better than the suggestion that he was a rolling stone. He would claim to have been married for thirty years only to have lost her to cancer or some such thing almost a decade ago. Women would like that.

He cupped Franka's chin roughly, forcing her head back so her face tilted upwards. She was gagged, just like the rest and blind to boot so she couldn't see the circle of victims and the barrels of chemicals around them.

Franka didn't bother to make a sound; there was nothing to be gained by it.

Next to her, Lubna Poelvoorde struggled against her bindings and wriggled her jaw to fight against the gag. The sight of her swollen eyes and tear-soaked face made Kurt smile. All they had to do was accept that they were beaten and they could have avoided the mess they now found themselves in.

Of course, it was her fault far more than it was Patrick's. It was his father's company and Patrick's poor decisions that had driven it to the point of insolvency. Had Patrick been wise enough to put his wife in charge they might have avoided ever crossing his radar.

Bending down to bring his face level with hers, Kurt gave her a sad, pitiful look. "Finally catching on, are you?"

She raged at him, her words contorted into nothing but noise by the gag in her mouth.

"You could have lived out the rest of your miserable lives in peace, but you chose to go digging instead. That cost Harold De Waele his life. Right here in this room as it happens, and then it cost his secretary her life, and now it is going to cost you yours."

She screamed in his face, her cheeks turning red and the veins in her forehead bulging.

"What's that?" he mocked her. "Oh, don't worry about me. I'll be on a beach in the Bahamas while they're still trying to identify your charred corpse."

Her eyes flared and she stopped talking, understanding now what the barrels were for.

Standing up, Kurt said, "The bits of it they find, that is." With his hands he mimed an explosion going off. "Not quite the same level as 9/11, but," he moved to stand behind a man tied to another chair directly opposite Lubna's, "thanks to this willing volunteer," the man bucked and fought his own bindings, "no one will be looking for me because Dirk De Graaf will be dead."

She hadn't noticed until now just how similar his features, age, shape, and haircut were to Dirk De Graaf's. Lubna had no idea that the man she could see was not Dirk De Graaf but an American imposter. Kurt Berger was getting ready to pull the exact same stunt he used to vanish the first time.

Billal and Medhi had proven just how capable and versatile they were by finding him a suitable double at short notice. Kurt hadn't bothered to learn the man's name; it made no difference. He had six sets of false passports plus matching driver's licenses, credit cards, and everything else he would need already in his suitcase. He would travel light; nothing more than a businessman taking a trip. He'd booked a return flight for the look of it, but was never coming back. When he landed, the first set of documents would go in the trash and the next set would take him to a new place. He would use a third set to get to his final destination in Nassau. He deserved a little sun after all the stress.

They would never find him, and he would leave behind no one who could tell the tale and expose him. Except for Erich Jannings, that is.

The old man who first exposed him remained a loose end that refused to be tied. Being spotted in the street by a man he hadn't seen in close to four decades was still such a random event it beggared belief. He worked under Erich as his junior, learning from him at Blench and Jones for almost a year. Erich had been wonderful; always generous with his time and forgiving of Kurt's inability to see the deals early enough to pounce on them. But as wonderful as he had been in 1985, Kurt didn't hesitate to order his murder for a second.

Now it looked as though he might live despite Kurt's best attempts to cut his life short.

Annoyed, because loose ends are what get people caught, Kurt called Jonas again. He'd been calling the idiot and his fool partner for more than two hours and could only conclude they were brighter than he thought and had chosen to abscond.

His plan had been to kill them both since they formed another loose end, but Kurt doubted they would be able to tell the police anything of any value if they were ever interrogated about Dirk De Graaf's movements and activities. He'd always held them at arm's length. Just like he did Billal and Medhi.

Bored playing with his victims, he went back to the task of arranging the barrels of chemicals. The fire would burn hot and the explosion would eliminate any forensic evidence. He would have to slice a few pieces off his double, otherwise the police would be able to identify him, but he'd done that before and such tasks had never bothered him.

Thinking thoughts of sun-drenched beaches and cocktails by the pool rather than wallowing in the circumstances that forced him to leave his empire in Antwerp, Kurt started to whistle a happy tune.

Chapter 49

E ndal remained confused about how they would know to get off until the
tram they were on drew close to Grote Markt. Her powerful nose began to
pick up the heavenly scent of the food when they were still half a kilometre away.

Rex grinned a big doggy grin at her. *"See?"*

*"And this is where we will find the strays you think will be able to lead us to where
we need to go?"*

Rex sure hoped so. If the concept of crossing his digits meant anything he would
have done so to the point of not being able to walk. This was a gamble, a throw
of the dice, and since it was the only one he had, there seemed no option but to
pretend it was all going to be fine and pray he was right.

Sounding utterly confident, Rex said, *"Yeah. Trust me."*

They were approaching the epicentre of Grote Markt and many of the passengers
were getting to their feet. The man Rex was sitting next to hadn't moved. When
Rex first took up position at his side, he looked down at him, looked around for
an owner, and decided to just let it be. The man was staying on, but Rex was
getting off, so he headed for the door with Endal following.

Following Rex's lead, Endal had found herself a mother with a little girl to sit by.
The girl stroked her head and scratched the fur around her shoulders, chatting
happily to her the whole journey. It made Endal question what it might have been
like to have a child in the house. Franka had pups of her own, but they were fully
grown now and visited only occasionally.

Leaving her on the tram, she gave one last look back and lost sight of the little girl's
face as she weaved between legs to get to the doors.

Bouncing down to pavement level, they moved away from the tram as the passengers disbursed and new ones got on. The air teemed with scents coming from dozens of food stalls, all of which were torturous to their canine brains.

"*I hate this place,*" Endal muttered. "*I always leave here so hungry I could eat a scabby cat.*"

Rex empathised; it was impossible to shut the food smells out and just as impossible to ignore them. However, he believed they were in the right place to find what they needed.

"*Remind me again what we are doing here.*"

Rex led Endal toward the market itself, talking over his shoulder. "*We need help and there are dogs here who know the city. I'm willing to bet they will know precisely where to find the combination of smells you described.*"

"*And you think they will help us?*"

Rex shot Endal a grin. "*Yeah, there's this hot little springer spaniel who's into me.*"

Approaching the market stalls, Rex spotted a tail poking out from under a canvas flap. Grinning slyly, he trotted over to it and placed a paw right on the tip.

"*Hey!*" The tail vanished so fast it was as though it had never been there, replaced in an instant by Shania's angry face. It softened when she saw who it was.

"*Oh, hey there, Big Boy.*"

Rex had a cool line ready to deliver, and fixed a sloppy smile on his face as he opened his mouth.

He wasn't expecting the slap.

"*Oh, yeah,*" Endal rolled her eyes. "*She's really into you.*"

Shania raised one eyebrow. "*Into you? Oh, really, Big Boy?*"

Rubbing his nose against his paw to scare the sting away, he whined, "*Why did you just hit me?*"

"*You told me you were unattached!*"

"I am unattached" Rex went cross-eyed trying to see if she had scratched his nose when she whacked it.

"Oh, yeah? So who is the sexy labrador I find you with? You think I can't smell your scent on her? You think I can't smell that you have been lying on the same carpet!"

Dumbfounded, Rex stammered, *"But ..."*

"Don't you but me, you doofus. And to think I was going to ... I hate dogs like you!" Shania spat venom. *"You go from girl to girl, never caring who you hurt. Saying whatever it will take to get them to give up the goods."* She shifted her eyes to look at Endal. *"Girlfriend, you need to lose this sack of cat vomit. All those promises he told you were lies."*

Endal was still reeling from the 'sexy' comment. She'd always thought of herself as big boned which everyone knew was a kinder term for something else.

"Um, I'm not sure what is happening here, or even who you are, but I am not mated with Rex. Never have been. We came here to recruit your help. My human has been kidnapped!"

More heads appeared from under the canvas flap. Plug, Jack, Russell, Fleabag and more all coming to check on the commotion.

"These domesticateds bothering you, Shania?" growled the Pitbull.

"Just say the word," snarled Fleabag, *"and we'll turn them into mincemeat."*

Rex glared at the bichon and was about to issue a challenge when Shania slapped his face again.

"Stop doing that!" he complained, holding his nose with both paws. *"Right on the tip. Both times."*

She scowled at him. *"Shush, you big doofus. That's your fault for failing to introduce the sexy labrador as your friend."*

"You didn't give me a chance!" Rex whined.

Shania slapped him again.

"Ow! Stop doing that!"

"I barely tapped you. Now stay quiet ... all of you. I want to hear what the labrador has to say."

Endal explained what happened to her human and the scents she detected on the two men.

"You want us to help you save a human?" Shania checked that she understood what was being asked. *"One of the species who took us in, gave us a home, then kicked us out because we left a puddle on the carpet, or got bigger and weren't so cute any longer."* All eyes swung to the Pitbull. *"Or because we set fire to the house and barked while it burned."* All eyes swung to the bichon who backed through the canvas leaving a yellow line behind. *"My point is, why should we?"*

Rex struggled to believe what he was hearing. Dogs help humans, that's just how it is. He could not imagine life without his human. To his way of thinking they were symbiotic, each bringing to the party that which the other didn't have.

Endal glared at Rex. They had wasted their time, time they didn't have.

Rex met her gaze with apologetic eyes. This outcome was one he could never have imagined.

A snigger cut through the air.

"Wow," laughed Shania, the other dogs starting to join in, *"You domestics are an easy mark."* She came out from under the canvas, the other dogs following. *"Come on. The place you want is down by the river. It's the only place that has those scents combined. We want the number eight tram!"*

With her final comment she started running, the pack of strays whipping out from under the canvas as more and more of them joined the adventure. Rex and Endal found themselves swept up in the race to get to the tram and not only did they suddenly have a destination, they had help too.

Chapter 50

A lbert felt absolute fatigue weighing him down like a lead suit. He'd left England to escape the fame and constant recognition recent events there had brought him. He wasn't escaping forever, just taking a break from it. He would go home for Christmas and was set to return to Europe a little while thereafter to visit a few places with Roy and Beverly, his neighbours from across the street.

After the rigours of his culinary tour around the British Isles, he felt certain he would find peace and solitude travelling through the European nations with Rex at his side, yet just a few days after leaving England, he was alone and potentially on his way to meet his doom.

Kurt had Franka and was going to kill her if Albert didn't surrender. He gave him a place to go to and warned what would happen if he didn't comply or was stupid enough to involve the authorities.

Ironically, there had been times in his police career when a person was taken hostage. He'd never been directly involved, but spoke with the officers who were. The person ordered to pay the ransom was always told not to contact the police and the police always let them know they did the right thing in ignoring the command.

Obviously, there had to be some who obeyed which the police therefore never knew about, so faced with the order to leave the police out of it, Albert needed about half a second to choose not to comply.

Kurt wasn't going to let Franka go and likely planned to kill Albert too. Meekly turning himself over would just get him killed along with everyone else.

He got into the taxi at the head of the queue, provided directions, and thumbed the number Margaret used to call him earlier. His choice to leave and then tell them what he was doing was calculated. They were going to try to talk him out of it, but if she could track his phone once, she could do it again. He was going to lead them right to De Graaf and whoever he was holding hostage.

The taxi dropped him on the corner of a street in Den Dam in the industrial north of the city. He looked around expecting to see someone waiting for him, and finding no one, settled against a wall to wait.

Less than a minute passed when a black Mercedes pulled to a stop at the kerb four feet from his toes. There were two Asian men in the front, the ones he'd formerly thought of as De Graaf's associates.

They said nothing when they exited the car and Albert half expected them to stun him again. They didn't, but they opened the back door as a wordless invite and when he stepped up to the car, they stopped him.

"Phone," demanded Billal.

Albert swallowed hard. So it wasn't just Margaret who knew people could be tracked with their smart device.

When he hesitated to hand it over, Billal gripped his coat and started to frisk. He found it soon enough, but Albert's worry it might go under his boot proved erroneous when the man holding it tossed it underhand into the back of a passing flatbed truck.

Now Margaret could follow it, probably with Bervoets and others in tow, but they would never find him.

He watched the van vanish in the flow of traffic following it, but that was the last thing he saw because a bag went over his head. Handled roughly, he was pushed into the car where his arms were zip tied behind his back.

One of them got in next to him, he could feel their weight on the bench seat to his left, then their hands when his head was forced down so no one would see them driving through town with a kidnap victim.

Albert told himself to stay calm and think, but the sense of worry wouldn't need much of a nudge to develop into full blown panic. His clever plan was going up in smoke.

He was still trying to devise a new strategy ten minutes later when the sound outside the car changed. Even without being able to see, he knew he was now inside. Inside somewhere big and open, like a warehouse. The air had a damp quality to it and there was something suppressing the sound from echoing the way it would if they were outside.

The bag was ripped from his head to leave Albert blinking in the harsh light.

Sunlight shone in from a set of sliding doors looking out onto the river. He was in an old industrial building of some sort, its original use no longer obvious though it looked to have been a factory of some kind – the floor was too clean and cared for to have been anything in the construction or engineering worlds.

The man on the backseat pushed him toward the door to get out though Albert had to wait for the driver to open it for him. They kept his hands zip tied behind his back, one of them holding his right arm just below the shoulder to steer him to a door in one wall.

On the other side, Albert saw a face he now recognised. Kurt Berger had his sleeves rolled up and a mild perspiration had formed on his brow despite the cool air.

He stopped what he was doing to look up at his latest captive, another piece of the puzzle that formed his escape to a new life.

Albert took in the scene just beyond the rich stockbroker where he spotted Franka. She was alive at least. Far from alone, there were three other people tied to chairs just as she was. Albert wondered who the other people could be.

One chair remained unoccupied.

"Mr Smith," Kurt Berger called, "why don't you come and join us?"

Chapter 51

"*This is the place?*" Rex stared at the dull, squat industrial building. It was just one of many in the area, most of which were still in use by businesses fixing cars or storing goods to be shipped to meet customer orders placed online or in a store miles away.

The building to their front stood apart from the others and was the last in line, backed up against the water where decades ago it shipped its goods out through sliding doors onto barges that would carry them downriver.

The pack was fanned out, more than two dozen dogs of every shape and size with their faces aimed at the same rundown building.

Endal sniffed deeply, holding the air in her nose until she was sure the scent profiles aligned.

"*Yes, this is what they smelled of.*"

It meant they were in the right place, but would need to get closer to find Franka if she was here. Just because the men smelled of this place didn't mean they returned here when they took her.

Rex sampled the air searching for a familiar scent; hoping he might detect one of the humans who took Franka. He had his own score to settle with them.

As a pack they crept forward, sticking to the shadows thrown by the afternoon sun and picking their way around discarded crates, pallets and old, rusty, machine parts.

Coming around to the west, they found an open door and inside that was the car. Neither Rex not Endal could say for certain it was the same car they chased earlier and seeing only in black and white the car's colour was lost to them. If they got close enough, they would be able to tell if Franka had been in it, and Rex could tell Endal was chomping at the bit to find her.

Rex turned to speak to Shania and the strays only to find most of them had wandered off.

"Where'd they all go?"

Shania was equally surprised to find her pack missing, but backtracking just a few feet revealed where they had gone: there was a food truck a hundred metres away. Set up to service the workers and visitors, it was set out with some old plastic tables and chairs. Men in high-vis vests chomped their way through belly busting sandwiches and burgers built to sustain a day of hard labour.

The strays had caught a whiff of it and were circling now, looking for a way to score themselves a meal. Rex needed to get them back, but before he asked Shania to round them up, he wanted to discuss how they were going to approach their objective.

A fence ran around the building's outer perimeter, an old chain link thing erected so long ago it was rusted down to nothing in places. Getting past it would present no trouble, but what then?

Rex wasn't one for boldly charging into a situation without a plan. Sometimes such a thing was necessary, but if they were in the right place, and they would know soon enough if they were not, he wanted a strategy. Otherwise he would be leading Endal, plus Shania and her pack against men with weapons and the odds were that someone would get hurt. Possibly worse than hurt.

Endal was less inclined to wait.

"It's my human, Rex. Not yours. I'm going in."

Rex knew he would feel the same if it was Albert they were talking about, but blocked Endal's path.

"We're all going, Endal. I just want to know what we are walking into, okay? We need a plan. Even if it's not a great plan."

Unable to contain her anxiety, Endal tried to go around Rex. She was broader across the shoulders and heavier set, which meant she would win in a shoving contest, but she certainly wasn't faster.

Rex dodged left and right, getting in Endal's way no matter which way she went.

Angry, Endal barked, *"Get out of my way!"* the sound echoed across the open ground, reverberating against the empty building to the background noise of a hundred pigeons taking flight.

His eyes twinkling, Rex said, *"Hold on. I've just had an idea."*

Chapter 52

A lbert received another shove, Billal pushing him to keep walking. Kurt was
thirty yards away.

"Franka, your father is alive and well," he called out, ignoring everyone else. He
wanted to add that he was awake and telling the police everything, but he wanted
to save that surprise for the right moment.

Franka raised her head, confirming that she was awake and alert. The gag prevented her from speaking, but she mumbled a response anyway.

"Not for long," quipped Kurt with a smile. "I will deal with Erich myself if I have
to."

Albert was halfway across the floor, Billal and Medhi following close behind like
shadows when a loud bark echoed in from outside.

Kurt's brow dipped into a questioning frown. "You brought the dog?"

Medhi said, "No. Of course not. He didn't have the dog with him when we picked
him up."

Albert knew it wasn't Rex barking, but said nothing. Instead he looked at Franka.
She couldn't exchange a wink, or give any other indication that she recognised
Endal's voice, and perhaps it wasn't hers. However, Albert had seen Rex pull off
stunts that defied explanation more than once and he'd been heading in this rough
direction when he last checked the App.

Kurt almost dismissed it, but caution and prudence had kept him safe all these
years; eliminate the risks before they can hurt you.

"Go check it out. Both of you," he nodded his head back toward the door.

"What about this one?" Billal grabbed Albert's arm again.

"Leave him. I think I can handle one old man. Mr Smith and I are going to have a little chat, aren't we, Albert?"

Albert returned the generous fake smile with interest. "Absolutely, Kurt. I think we should."

Kurt's smile locked in place, his facial muscles rigid while his eyes turned cold.

Billal and Medhi looked at each other, neither having any clue what had just happened and wondering if the other might.

"I said, go," Kurt reminded them. "If his dog is here, kill it." Kurt liked dogs, but the time for being nice was long gone.

Albert's hands were still tied behind his back, so he sauntered forward, making his stride look casual as he looked about for anything he might be able to use to get them free. Right now it was just him and Kurt. With the brothers gone, for a short while at least, he stood an outside chance of overpowering him.

If his hands were free.

It was a long shot, but all he had to do was knock him down. Then he could free the others and they could all get out.

To distract his 'host' Albert said, "Did you kill Dirk De Graaf in 9/11 or was he already dead?"

"No, no, I killed him. He was injured but I beat him to death with a piece of stationery equipment. I'd never killed anyone before, but I have to tell you, it was really easy. I thought it might keep me awake at night, but it never has."

"Yes, you seem like a complete sociopath," Albert replied. He was getting close, just a couple of yards shy, but there was nothing around he could see that would help his situation. He wanted an old screwdriver left behind years ago. Or an iron bar. Anything he could use to get leverage against the zip tie.

"Name calling, Albert? You think you can bother me with insults? I expected better from you." He waited for Albert to show interest before continuing with, "Yes, I looked you up. When I discovered the name of the man who was proving to be such a thorn in my side, I knew there was something familiar about it. After such success, what is it like to fail?"

Albert smiled in Kurt's face, a bemused grin to indicate he knew things Kurt did not.

"You think I have failed?"

"Well, you're about to die along with these other fools, so, yes, I think I would count that as a fail."

"Do you recall the name Margaret Bloomfield?"

Kurt's expression froze again.

"I see that you do," Albert made his way to the one remaining chair and settled into it. "She is here in Antwerp, Kurt, and she knows you killed Dirk De Graaf to escape her in 2001."

Kurt's face portrayed abject horror. Complete shock. Until he started to laugh.

"Oh, that's priceless. I mean well done for figuring so much out. I must say you are quite the detective, but I'm about to vanish, Albert. These barrels," he indicated around the circle, "are filled with a highly flammable chemical. Dirk De Graaf is about to perish for the second time and if they ever do figure out the body wearing my clothes isn't mine, they still won't be able to find me. I'm sorry Albert, but this is a swing and a miss from you."

The sound of footsteps approaching changed in volume when Billal and Medhi came through the door from the outer area to the inner.

Medhi reported, "There're some dogs over by the food truck, boss. Looks like a bunch of strays. Nothing to worry about."

No longer able to discuss his plan to leave and never come back now that Billal and Medhi could hear him, Kurt clapped his hands together. "Right, I guess it's time to get this show on the road."

Lubna, Patrick, and the poor, innocent man off the street all began to squirm and fight against their bindings again. They yelled behind their gags, only Franka remaining calm as though she had accepted her fate.

"Oh, don't worry," Kurt said, "The brothers are going to shoot you all first. I'm not completely ruthless."

It was news to the brothers, but they drew their guns and walked around to join their boss.

Kurt lit a match. Holding it carefully so it would burn but not too fast, he crab-walked two places to his right where he lit a pile of rags. Making sure the brothers were facing the captives and not him, he then drew his own gun, lining it up on the back of Medhi's head.

It was a shame he couldn't take them with him, they had been so loyal, but framing them for his own murder was a better solution. He would leave a large bag of cash in their car to make it look like they had double crossed him and they were the ones clearing house. Their own deaths would be unexplained to give the police a fun conundrum to decipher, and whatever conclusion they drew they would still not find Kurt Berger because he ceased to exist twenty-three years ago.

He was about to give the command for the brothers to shoot, and ready to kill them the moment they had, when a dog appeared.

It was a tiny grey fluffball, a bichon frise Kurt thought, though it needed a really good bath and a day at the doggy salon. It had something in its mouth and was running flat out in their direction.

No sooner had he spotted that than a second dog appeared. This one was a scruffy Jack Russell cross of some kind. Just like the bichon it was carrying something in its mouth.

Kurt's eyebrows wiggled in confusion.

A third then fourth dog appeared right on the heels of the first two. It was bizarre and they were all carrying something though they were moving too fast for anyone to be able to make out what it was.

Until the bichon reached Medhi's feet and spat it out, that is. The dog didn't stop, it just kept on running, tearing across the factory floor to get to the open sliding doors on the other side.

The Jack Russell cross and the two dogs following it did the same thing, dropping what they held at Medhi's feet or Billal's feet and then finally Kurt's feet.

Kurt looked down at the half a burger.

When he looked back up he found Medhi and Billal looking at him. They should have been looking at the captives, but they were not and the question Kurt knew they were about to ask would have nothing to do with the dogs or the food they just delivered like some kind of strange canine version of Uber Eats.

"What's with the gun, boss?" Billal asked, his own weapon now pointing roughly toward the man he knew as Dirk De Graaf.

Medhi had a pretty good idea what his boss had planned for them, but before he could raise his gun to strike first, the sound of a thousand pigeons filled the air.

Chapter 53

Three seconds had passed since the first dog dropped his mouthful of food. It took Rex some time to convince the strays this was the plan they needed. It was not in their nature to pass up on a free meal, but the pigeons provided the tool he needed to get them all in and out without anyone getting shot.

They mugged a pair of builders when they got their order from the food truck, rushing them to trip and topple their trays. The bigger dogs grabbed the food and ran, curse words and rocks from the ground peppering their retreat.

Then Rex had to protect it because the strays were salivating and so desperate to eat it he had to promise them a feast of their own if they could just play along. He had no clue how he would deliver the feast but that was a problem for later.

Getting the pigeons to follow the food was easy. The four voluntolds (Shania didn't them an option) had to carry it into the factory, spit it out so the pigeons saw it, wait for them to descend, them snatch it back up and run like the wind.

They all knew what a gun was so Rex told them to drop the food next to anyone who had a gun.

Outside, Rex, Endal, Shania, and her pack listened and hoped. The sound of the pigeons giving chase, a thousand pairs of wings flapping manically was not a noise that could be mistaken for anything else. The moment the pigeons took flight, the dogs started running.

They barked and whooped, filling the air with their excitement as they charged through the old factory letting their noses lead them to where they needed to be.

Rex picked up Franka's smell first, but only because he was looking for it. When he then caught Albert's in the next breath, he increased his pace. He'd been worried about the old man for hours, but trying to do the right thing for Endal, and knowing Albert would want to rescue Franka just as much as he would, Rex pushed thoughts of his own human from his head.

Yet he was here, and that meant Rex could achieve everything he wanted if his plan worked the way he wanted.

The door from the factory outer areas to the inner part where the humans and pigeons were currently locked in a deadly aerial battle caused a pinch point that slowed the dogs down. Not for long though, the pack diving through the gap to fan out on the other side.

The pigeons had just about exhausted the supply of food and were already beginning to depart. The humans were covered in feathers and coated in poop. All of them, not just the three with the guns. They had been blinded by feathers for the last twenty seconds, those with their arms free flailing them in the air to protect their faces.

Rex knew the men by sight as well and smell, but the rest of the pack did not. He wasn't the fastest among them; many of the small dogs had already reached the targets. So although he barked instructions, Rex could not be sure if the strays would be aware enough to attack the right people.

With the pigeons leaving, the armed men were recovering and if the lead dogs didn't take them down, they were going to start shooting.

It was a lucky thing then that Billal, Medhi, and Kurt Berger were standing where Albert, Franka, and some others were sitting. It made them easy to pick out.

Billal was the first to go down, Plug the Pitbull running through his shins to 'cat flap' him with a bark of triumph. By the time his body hit the factory floor and a dozen dogs descended on him, his brother, Mehdi, was suffering a similar fate.

Growls, barks, and snarls drowned out the human wailing and neither man got a shot off. The strays grabbed limbs, biting hard and shaking their heads. Individually, most of the dogs were too small to do any real harm, but combined they were more than a match for the brothers.

Kurt got a shot off, missing his target, but doing enough to dissuade the strays from coming at him. Standing five metres behind the others, he got just enough extra warning and was backing away when Billal and Medhi went down beneath a seething canine blanket.

Albert saw the brothers' guns fall free. They hadn't been able to keep hold of them with so many dogs biting their arms. It came as a relief, but not so much as seeing Rex emerge through the pack.

The fire was growing, the heat from it already uncomfortable for Albert who was closest. He turned to offer Rex his back and craning his neck to look over one shoulder said, "Here, boy, bite through this will you?"

Rex didn't understand the request at first, but seeing his human's hands clamped together by a piece of plastic, he set to work.

Albert's hands came free with a jolt. His shoulders were sore from being locked in the same position for too long, but there was no time to massage life back into them. They needed to leave. Acutely aware Kurt had chosen to flee, Albert peered through the mounting smoke to spot him running for the river.

Kurt had his head down and his limbs pumping. The fire was lit and burning, the pile of rags transferring their flames to the first barrel in line. Soon they would all be ablaze and shortly thereafter the whole building would explode. If the darned dogs were still inside so much the better.

Endal went straight to Franka. The human threat had been eliminated and she had always been her sole focus.

"*I'm here,*" she nuzzled her lap and jumped up to lick her face.

With her hands tied behind the chair, Franka could do nothing to protect herself from Endal's affections, but they came free a moment later when Albert cut through them.

He'd finally spotted something he could use – one half of an old, broken pair of scissors – when he was talking to Kurt. When the first dogs appeared with the food, he knew Rex had to be behind it, once again proving how remarkable he could be.

Rex was fussing around him now, just as overjoyed to be reunited as Albert was.

Leaving Franka to return Endal's affections now that her hands were free, Albert moved to the next person. He cut through his bindings so the man could remove his gag and handed him the rusty half scissor.

"Here, get the others free and get out of here!" It was getting warm to say the least, the fire spreading from barrel to barrel. The flames still burned around the outside, but the contents would be heating up and he had no intention of still being around when they hit critical point.

Shania barked to get her pack moving, "*Everyone out!*" There was real panic in her words. The fire was terrifying and the threat had been eliminated. The humans were almost free and it was time to be somewhere else.

Rex stood by Albert's side when the strays began to head for the exit. They went back the way they had come, the opposite direction from Kurt and he was torn with what he was supposed to do now.

Shania hesitated long enough to make sure all her strays were leaving, then barked to get Rex moving too.

"*What are you doing? We have to go! This whole place is going to blow!*"

Rex looked up at his human.

Albert's focus was on Billal and Medhi. The brothers were holding each other up, both limping for the exit with blood dripping from their fingers, they had so many bites. Their guns were on the ground, abandoned in the heat of the dog pack attack.

He strode across the factory floor, collecting one and then the other, so he held one in each hand, ready at his sides.

Shania barked again. "*Rex! Let's go!*"

He looked her way. His human was making no attempt to get out, so even though he could feel the heat of the fire crisping his fur, Rex was going nowhere.

"*I'm sorry, Shania. I have to stay.*"

"*For a human?*"

"*No, not for a human. For my human.*"

Shania gave up. She'd helped Rex and involved her pack because it was the right thing to do, but her strays had already fled, she was the last one left. Only her, Endal and Rex remained with the humans still fighting to get free.

She gave Rex one last look, then ran for the distant sunlight.

Albert checked each of the handguns, ejecting the magazines to check they were fully loaded and refitting them once more so they were ready to fire.

Cutting through Lubna's ties, Patrick Poelvoorde yelled, "What are you going to do?"

Albert's jaw was already set with a hard expression. He was far too old to be doing the things he did, and given a choice he wouldn't do them. There was no choice though, so with determined eyes, made to look mad by the dancing flames around him, Albert growled, "I'm going to stop a criminal."

Chapter 54

"Rex!" Albert had watched Kurt Berger escape the building twenty seconds ago. He was moving too fast for Albert to catch, but sending Rex after him was a whole different proposition.

Obediently, Rex fell by his human's left leg, fairly sure he knew where they were going and very much ready to do his part. He stopped two paces later, ducking and spinning to go back for something.

"*Endal!*" he barked. The room was beginning to get smoky, the acrid fumes from the barrels anything but pleasant.

The humans were in a gaggle, Patrick and Lubna working on the final set of bindings that tied Kurt's body double to the chair.

Endal twisted around to face Rex. "*This is intense!*"

"*It sure is, but listen, I'm going after the bad guy. This is your chance. If you ever want to do something exciting, you will never get a better shot than this!*"

"*I have to look after Franka.*"

"*Bring her with you!*"

Endal's paws moved, but only to turn her around. She dearly wanted to go with Rex, but her human would always come first.

"Rex!" Albert shouted to be heard above the increasing din of the fire.

Rex started moving, giving his friend one last look. "*I have to go. Get to safety!*" Pushing off from his back legs, Rex twisted his body around to face the river and put his head down. It was chase and bite time.

Endal watched, mesmerised by the athletic German Shepherd, his silky coat flowing sinuously like water with each powerful bound.

"Endal! Endal get us out of here! There's my wonderful dog!" Franka could smell, feel, and hear the fire. The smoke was starting to tickle her throat and she was anxious to be anywhere else.

Patrick and Lubna got Kurt's body double free with a shout of triumph.

He screamed, "Let's go!" grabbing Franka and hoisting her into his arms in one move as he started forward.

"*Hey! That's my human!*" Endal barked, running after the humans.

They passed Billal and Medhi who were still limping painfully at the best speed they could manage. When they got through the door and could see the tempting open air beyond the factory walls, Endal stopped. She could see the humans were going to carry Franka to safety. Just as Rex said, if she was ever going to do something exciting, it had to be right now.

Questioning her sanity, she barked a battle cry and turned back toward the small inferno now dominating the middle of the factory. She gave it a wide birth, bounding across the dirty concrete floor to get out the other side. Bursting into daylight, next to the river she turned right and followed Rex's scent.

A hundred yards ahead of her, Rex was closing in on Kurt. The American's head start hadn't lasted long and he was flagging already, his body not able to sustain the speed he needed it to produce.

Rex knew the game was over. He could slow to a canter and still catch his quarry, but Albert hadn't given the command to 'Sic 'im', and Rex wasn't sure what he was supposed to do. Should he just take the man down anyway?

He turned to look back the way he had come. Albert was coming as fast as he could, but looking in his direction, Rex saw a streaking golden blob of fur coming up fast.

Endal passed Albert doing twice the speed of sound, or so it seemed to her. She rarely got to run anywhere and this was the second time today she'd needed to test her top speed.

"Rex! Rex, I'm coming!"

Rex slowed a little more, taking his eyes off the target which was a big mistake.

Kurt could hardly get any air into his lungs. His whole scheme was going wrong all because of an old man and his annoying dog. He didn't know whether the Poelvoordes had escaped, but he was willing to bet they had. He could see Albert Smith giving chase and if he was free the others had to be.

Lining up his gun, he took aim and fired.

Rex jumped half out of his skin when the bullet cracked over his head. He also ran into cover, getting behind an old concrete bollard that lined the river's edge.

Kurt took aim again, this time at Albert Smith, but his second shot was as wild as the first. He was too out of breath to keep his arm steady enough.

Albert stepped into cover too, hugging the building where a steel column provided a hiding place.

Endal simply powered on. Too full of pent-up energy and aggression that required an outlet, she ignored a bullet when it kicked up chips of concrete two yards in front of her face.

Rex barked, *"Take cover, you fool!"* but Endal paid no heed.

She passed Rex, her ears flapping magnificently in the breeze her speed created.

Fearing for her, Rex came out of cover too, running behind the mad labrador.

Kurt took aim again, this time using another of the bollards to steady his arms. He sighted on Endal's skull and started to squeeze the trigger.

Chapter 55

M argaret was just getting out of the car when the chemicals ignited in what could only be described as a spectacular fireball. The factory was thankfully bereft of glass windows except in the office area, but those blew out into the river and all but one of the sky lights in the roof elected to make a bid for the outer atmosphere.

The shockwave threw a wall of dust and detritus outward, peppering the police as they arrived.

Lieutenant Filip Bervoets was slower to leave his car than Margaret, avoiding the hairdryer effect, but he had opened the driver's door and caught it with his face when the blast tried to close it again. Getting out with a hand holding his nose, he looked at the ruined building in horror.

"That's where they are?" he asked Margaret in a tone that denoted he didn't want it to be true.

Margaret didn't answer. Like Bervoets she was horrified. The building's structure was intact, but there was little chance it remained sound. Flames licked out through the holes in the roof and could be seen through the open doors at the front.

"Are you looking for us?" asked Lubna, taking charge as she always did.

Margaret, Lieutenant Bervoets, and the half dozen cops that came with them spun around to find four dirty, smoke-stained people approaching from behind them. Franka had her hand hooked into Patrick's elbow, letting him guide her as they made their way back toward the burning factory.

When they escaped it, they didn't stop running until they reached the food truck. There they met the builders who were feeding Shania and her strays. Rather than be angry about losing their food, the duo they mugged simply ordered more and when the strays reappeared they took pity on them.

The builders were watching now, enjoying the unexpected show while they devoured their snacks and threw titbits to the dogs.

Pointing at Billal and Medhi, who made it out of the factory just before it blew but looked like refugees from a plane crash, Lubna added, "You may wish to arrest those two. They took us from our house at gunpoint and were going to kill us."

A nod from Bervoets was all it took to get the uniformed officers running in the right direction. They had heard what Lubna said and were about to move anyway.

The Iranian brothers offered no resistance. They had no fight left in them.

"Frau Schweiger," Lieutenant Bervoets could hardly believe what he was seeing. "How did you get out of the factory?"

Margaret threw in a question of her own, "And why does my tracking app claim your phone is still inside it?"

"Probably because it is," Franka guessed. "It was taken off me and I think Kurt Berger used it to call Albert. Albert?" she called out, concerned that she was yet to hear his voice. "Albert, are you there?"

"Sorry, no, Franka," Margaret replied. "He's not here. Didn't he get out with the rest of you?"

This time Lubna answered. "He went after Dirk De Graaf or Kurt Berger or whatever his name is. What's going on with that anyway?"

The explanation would take a while and outside the burning factory was neither the right time nor the right place. No one felt inclined to answer her anyway, they were all looking at the inferno that was the old factory and very deliberately not speculating on the survival prospects of anyone standing too close when it exploded.

An eerie silence fell, punctuated only by the sound of the fire devouring anything combustible.

Then a cough. It came from within the swirling smoke and dust to the right of the factory. All heads turned that way, the police, former FBI agent Margaret

Blookfield, Franka, the Poelvoordes, Kurt's unfortunate and still very bewildered body double, the builders, and all the stray dogs trained their eyes in the direction of the sound and thus were looking the right way when Kurt Berger stumbled out of the smoggy haze.

Lieutenant Bervoets' instant reaction was to go for his gun, but his hand stopped short when he saw that not only were Kurt's hands empty, they were raised.

The smoke swirled again, obscuring the rich stockbroker only to reveal him a moment later being flanked by Rex and Endal, both looking pleased with themselves, and then Albert, holding a gun in each hand like he was Clint Eastwood come to collect a bounty.

"*Was that everything you wanted?*" Rex asked.

Endal smiled wistfully. "*I think it was right for me. I'm glad I didn't bite him. I believe it would have plagued my dreams.*"

The bullet aimed at her head missed when the exploding factory threw Endal sideways. It did the same thing to Rex, both dogs narrowly missing a swim when their scrabbling paws found enough purchase to keep them on the quayside. Kurt lost his gun when he fell over, and Albert, tucked into the shell of a tall steel column, avoided the blast completely. Well, completely if one ignored the ringing in his ears.

Temporary tinnitus aside, he was relieved to be in one piece and to have made it through the smoke and dust to find Kurt lying on the ground drenched in dog pee. It was too much to have come from one animal, which meant both Endal and Rex chose to express their opinion in the least violent manner they could find.

It amused Albert no end.

Bervoets sent officers forward to take Berger into custody. He was still struggling not to think of him as De Graaf, but his name didn't matter all that much. The forensic crime guys had called while he was powering across Antwerp with Margaret in his passenger seat. They were just breaking the tip of the iceberg but described what they were finding as the greatest stock tampering empire they had ever heard of.

Bervoets suspected the Americans would want to take him back to the states to stand trial for his crimes there, even though he suspected his crimes in Belgium over the past twenty plus years would be far worse, but all that was far above his paygrade.

Albert watched the officers cuff Kurt, then flipped the two guns around in one fluid motion so he held them by the barrels – he didn't need or want them anymore.

Approaching, Lieutenant Bervoets instructed another officer to, "Disarm Mr Smith," and saw to it the guns were taken as evidence.

While he dealt with that, Margaret walked across to Kurt Berger. He was dripping wet in places, and looked both angry and miserable at the same time. Albert watched, curious to hear what she might have to say.

She said nothing. Instead, she went around behind his back where she grabbed his right arm and making 'Ewww' noises as she handled his damp clothing, she pushed his shirt sleeve up to reveal his skin.

"No tattoo," she remarked – it was the final confirmation if one was even needed. Taking a second to wipe her hands on a dry part of his shirt, she walked around the cops holding his arms. Pausing to look Kurt directly in his eyes, she said, "Goodbye, Kurt."

His mouth curled into a sneer, but Margaret was already walking away. The cops gave his arms a yank and Albert watched with satisfaction as they took him to a waiting squad car.

Margaret looked Albert up and down. "I think I owe you a drink."

"I would accept that offer."

Endal spotted Franka and took off. Like everyone else in the area, she was coming to see Albert.

"I think we owe you more than a drink," said Lubna.

"Our lives, perhaps," suggested Patrick.

Albert waved them off. "I'm just glad you all got out okay."

Endal gummed at Franka's wrists and fussed until she calmed her down. She'd wanted some excitement in her life, but the time spent away from Franka had cured her. She planned to never be out of her human's sight again.

Curious about one thing, Albert asked, "How did you find me? They threw my phone in the back of a truck."

"Oh, yes," Margaret started to dig around in her handbag. "We would have been here sooner, but that really threw us." She produced his phone, handing it over to Albert's great surprise.

"Thank you. But ..."

"But how did we find you if your phone was halfway across Antwerp?" Margaret had a big, knowing smile on her face. "I tracked Franka's instead, silly. Are all Brits this slow?" She was teasing him, and he was fine with it. She came to his rescue, and the fact that he hadn't needed to be saved diminished her effort and intentions not one bit.

He was tired, he needed a bath, and her offer of a drink really was something he wanted to cash in. Hoping there would be no reason why he couldn't return to his hotel, he looked around for Rex.

His dog had wandered off, but he hadn't gone far. He was talking to Shania and the strays, all of whom were about to skedaddle. The police were there and that meant animal services wouldn't be far away.

"*Will I see you again?*" Shania asked.

Rex nuzzled her ears. "*I don't think that's how this works. I will always be by my human's side, and you will always be here.*"

"*You could come back,*" she suggested hopefully.

"*And I cannot guarantee that I won't. But it seems unlikely. I think this is goodbye.*"

She looked into Rex's eyes for a while, soul gazing him until Plug the Pitbull shouted, "*Hey, Shania. It's time to go!*"

Rex nodded toward the pack of strays meandering back toward the city centre.

"*You should go.*"

And so she went, looking back only once, just before she was lost from sight.

Chapter 56

A lbert hung around for one more day, clearing things up with the police and providing them with a comprehensive statement that covered everything from the time Erich Jannings got on the tram to the point where he handed Kurt Berger over.

He went to visit Erich in his hospital bed with Franka and Jean. He couldn't take Rex in with him and wasn't going to leave him in the hotel again – Matthias and Jonas were yet to be caught – but Franka suggested a neighbour who would sit both dogs at her house.

Erich was bright and full of vigour when he and Albert finally met. He couldn't remember blurting Kurt Berger's name at Albert, but could recall meeting the brash young American in 1985. He was assigned as his mentor, helping Kurt to learn the business before the firm would assign him his own accounts. The picture in his photograph album where he stood next to Dirk De Graaf was, in fact, Kurt. Erich had never met Dirk De Graaf and being fairly new in Antwerp had never even heard of him.

Albert stayed chatting with him for two hours, listening while Franka regaled her father with all that he'd missed and how lucky they had been to survive in the end.

The papers were all over it, though at Albert's request his name had been kept a secret. He wasn't sure how long that would last – there were too many cops who knew about his involvement to hope that it would never get out, but he'd left England to escape the attention and wanted nothing from anyone other than the right to be left alone.

With Lieutenant Bervoets' help Albert was able to identify Jonas and Matthias, and it was nice to finally be able to put names to Erich's attackers. They were career criminals known to the police, but they had gone to ground and could well have left the city though Bervoets didn't credit them as smart enough to think of that.

Wherever they were, the duo would be licking their wounds and would show up somewhere in six months or a year. There were arrest warrants out for them, so it was just a matter of time before they too were caught.

On what proved to be his final morning in Antwerp, Albert came down for breakfast with Rex to find Margaret sitting in the hotel's plush lobby. She rose to her feet the moment she saw them, greeting Albert with a warm smile.

"I wanted to say goodbye before I left. I don't suppose you'll ever find yourself in Texas, and I have a lot to thank you for."

Albert wasn't so sure he agreed. What had he actually done? Erich stumbled across Kurt Berger, Rex chased off Jonas and Matthias. Franka made the call that brought Margaret into the picture to identify Dirk De Graaf as an imposter. Albert felt his contribution consisted mostly of shuttling back and forth to the hospital, but he thanked Margaret for her kind words and let her pull him into a brief hug.

Rex frowned. *"Hey, what about me?"*

Breaking the hug, Margaret ruffled the fur on Rex's head, and crouched to give him a hug too. He reminded her of a dog she'd had as a child and found herself questioning if retirement might be the ideal time to get a new one.

She repeated her goodbye and was gone, but waiting for his breakfast to be served, Albert thought about something she had said.

"Texas," he rolled the word around in his mouth. "Maybe when I am done in Europe, there might be cause for one more trip. I've heard everything is bigger in America."

Rex scratched behind his ear with a back foot. *"Makes no difference to me, old man. Is that where we are going next?"*

Giving Rex a pat, Albert said, "That's for another time though. Today we are going to France. I want to check out something called a Bretzel.

The End

Book 2 is waiting for you. Scan the QR code with your phone to find your copy of Old School.

Author's Notes:

H ello, Dear Reader,

Thank you for reading all the way to the end of this tale and beyond. I first started writing Albert Smith in 2020. It was the middle of lockdown, not that I really noticed the world going sideways in my log cabin at the bottom of the garden, and I was looking for a new series of cozy mysteries to capitalise on the success of my Patricia Fisher books.

I performed some research, reading into the books doing well in a subgenre called 'culinary cozy mystery'. The stories are the usual murder mystery tales one expects but they come with a culinary lilt, such as the sleuth is also a chef.

My research revealed some very obvious tropes and to follow them to meet reader expectations, I needed to write a female central protagonist whose spouse worked in law enforcement and had recently been killed in the line of duty. A year or so on from that tragedy, she would move, probably to a seaside resort where she would open a cupcake shop.

I am generalising, but genuinely not stretching things too far from the truth.

That sounded boring, so I chose instead to write a curmudgeonly man in his late seventies. He wouldn't be able to cook at all and the culinary element was to come from his desire to replicate some of his late wife's excellent cooking.

The Rex element ticked another box because there also exists another subgenre called 'animal cozy mystery'. However, the truth behind his character is a tale almost three decades in the making. In the nineties, I read a story in National Geographic about a man whose dog had been injured. Left quadriplegic, the advice was to euthanise. The owner chose instead to buy a Winnebago, fit it out with a specially designed hammock, and take the dog on a tour of the United States.

Together, man and dog spent months on the road visiting some of their nation's greatest treasures until the dog's health deteriorated and his end could no longer be avoided. The story stuck with me, rattling around in my head and going through several iterations before coalescing into the Albert and Rex duo you have come to know and love.

I had to decide what to do about accents and whether I would have the locals in each location employ their own language from time to time. I toiled over this for months, in fact, before deciding to simply go with English.

I find the danger in employing accents is that the meaning I wish to impart might not always come through. It also makes audiobook creation a nightmare. Since most of the characters will be local, there would be whole swathes of dialogue needing to be written with an accent. I hope the end result works for you.

Before you go any farther, there are spoilers below, so if you read these notes before you read the book (which is what my mother does) then I advise not doing so on this occasion.

In this story I write about Albert's body and the sense of decrepitude he sometimes feels. In my mid-fifties I am very aware that I am no longer able to perform the same physical feats I could just a decade or so ago. I was one of those kids who was in an athletics club when my age still ran to single figures. Then it was swimming and when I joined the army at seventeen I was one of the fit people they had playing every sport under the sun. Consequently I have no knees, my elbow joints are those of a seventy-year-old, my back is far from great, and my shoulders are terrible. I can only imagine what I will be like in another twenty years and try to write Albert's maladies with a sensitive, sympathetic tone.

One of my wonderful assistants remarked on some of the character names employed in this story. I cannot comment on where other authors find their names, but I get mine from old or current Hollywood actors. Constantly having to devise new names, I try my very best to keep them diverse. In a story I wrote not so long ago, I melded two subplots and to my horror discovered the tale contained two Edwards. There was nothing much I could do about it; the characters were already established in other books. I changed one to Eddie, but it remained confusing. Hoping to prevent that from happening again, I vary my names as much as possible. They are all taken from two or three real people, their first and last names swapped about to create something new.

Endal was a real dog. I read about him in the nineties. Trained to be an assistance dog, he became the be-all and end-all of an injured serviceman's life. Endal was able to respond to over one hundred instructions as well as a very large number ("hundreds") of signed commands. He could retrieve items from supermarket shelves, operate buttons and switches, and load and empty a washing machine. He was able to put a card into a cash machine, retrieve the card when the process was complete, and return the card to a wallet.

Endal came to national attention in a 2001 incident, when his human was knocked out of his wheelchair by a passing car outside a hotel. Endal pulled him into the recovery position, retrieved his mobile phone from beneath the car, retrieved a blanket from the upturned wheelchair and covered him, alert barked at a nearby hotel for assistance with no result, and then ran into the hotel to obtain help.

He is my guiding principle when I want Rex to do something and question if I am just being unrealistic. In this story, Rex boards a tram by himself, befriends some strays, and leads an attack to rescue captive humans using pigeons to create a diversion. It is fiction, but I genuinely don't think I am stretching things all that far.

I hope you enjoyed it because there is a whole lot of adventure still to come.

Take care.

Steve Higgs

What's Next for Albert and Rex?

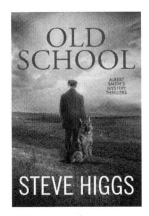

Sometimes the oldest secrets are the hardest ones to keep.

When a retired police detective and his dog wander into a small town in the French mountains, no one expects the trouble they will uncover.

A body has been unearthed at a nearby archaeological dig and it's clear no one was ever supposed to find it. The locals deny all knowledge; they have no idea who it could be, but there is something disturbing about how they all give the exact same answer.

And what of the archaeologists? What were they really looking for? It isn't the Stone Age settlement they claim to be after. Does everyone in this town have a secret they don't want exposed?

Together with his trusted sidekick, Albert and Rex are going to get to the bottom of the mystery.

He could walk away, there's nothing to make him investigate. But Albert Smith has an old school way of thinking, and he's got nothing better to do.

History of the Dish

I n English-speaking countries, Belgian waffles are a variety of waffle with a lighter batter, larger squares, and deeper pockets than American waffles. Belgian waffles were originally leavened with yeast, but baking powder is now often used. They are often eaten as a breakfast food; toppings vary from whipped cream, confectioners' sugar, soft fruit, and chocolate spread, to syrup and butter or margarine. They may also be served with vanilla ice cream and fresh fruit (such as strawberries) as a dessert.

In Belgium itself, there are several kinds of waffle, including the Brussels waffle and the Liège waffle.

Originally showcased in 1958 at Expo 58 in Brussels, Belgian waffles were introduced to the United States by a Belgian named Walter Cleyman at the Century 21 Exposition in Seattle in 1962, and served with whipped cream and strawberries. The waffles were further popularized in the United States during the 1964 New York World's Fair at in , New York City. These waffles were introduced by Maurice Vermersch of Brussels, Belgium. Largely based on a simplified recipe for the Brussels waffles, Vermersch decided to change the name to the Bel-Gem Waffle upon observing that many Americans could not correctly identify Brussels as the capital of Belgium. These waffles were served with whipped cream and strawberries, and they were sold for a dollar.

Recipe

I ngredients:

All-purpose flour — plain flour is perfect for waffle batter for creating tender waffles with a crispy exterior.

Baking powder — When paired with whipped egg whites, this leavening agent creates tiny air pockets throughout the batter, making super fluffy waffles.

Milk — feel free to use any percentage of dairy milk or any unsweetened plant-based milk you prefer.

Neutral oil — I typically reach for vegetable or canola oil, but avocado or grapeseed will also work beautifully.

Eggs — you'll need to separate the yolks and whites (yolks add tenderness, while whipped whites add fluffiness). I prefer separating them cold as the egg white is a bit thicker, and the yolk is less likely to break.

Vanilla extract — for added richness and warmth. Feel free to swap in an equal amount of vanilla paste or powder, or use half as much ground vanilla bean instead.

Method:

1. Preheat your Belgian waffle iron. In a large bowl, whisk together the flour, baking powder, sugar, and salt.

2. In a medium bowl, whisk together the milk, oil, egg yolks, and vanilla together.

3. Stir the wet ingredients into the dry ingredients until almost combined.

4. In a separate mixing bowl, beat the egg whites on high speed until stiff peaks form.

5. Gently fold the egg whites into the waffle batter until no streaks remain.

6. Scoop about 1/3 cup of Belgian waffle batter for each waffle. (This will depend on the size and settings of your waffle maker, so feel free to experiment with amounts.) Cook according to the manufacturer's instructions. Serve hot with butter, syrup, berries, whipped cream, or your favourite toppings.

Pro tips:

Start with cold eggs. Separate the eggs while cold from the fridge so the egg yolks are less likely to break. Additionally, I recommend using a 3-bowl system — 1 bowl for your freshly separated egg white, 1 bowl for the yolks, and 1 bowl to pour the whites into. That way, if a yolk breaks into one white, it doesn't ruin the whole batch!

Use a clean mixing bowl. Make sure your equipment is squeaky clean before whipping the egg whites to lofty clouds. Any lingering oils from previous baking adventures will prevent them from setting into stiff peaks. If you're not sure, I suggest running a cotton ball dipped in lemon juice on your beaters and bowl to clean them.

Preheat the waffle iron. A crispy waffle is created in part from the batter, but most importantly from the hot iron. Turn it on before you start mixing up your batter so it's nice and hot when you're ready to start cooking. If you can choose settings on your Belgian waffle maker, I recommend opting for a darker setting to achieve a crispier waffle.

Free Books and More

Want to see what else I have written? Go to my website.

https://stevehiggsbooks.com/

Or sign up to my newsletter where you will get sneak peeks, exclusive giveaways, behind the scenes content, and more. Plus, you'll be notified of Fan Pricing events when they occur and get exclusive offers from other authors because all UF writers are automatically friends.

Click the link or copy it carefully into your web browser.

https://stevehiggsbooks.com/newsletter/

Prefer social media? Join my thriving Facebook community.

Want to join the inner circle where you can keep up to date with everything? This is a free group on Facebook where you can hang out with likeminded individuals and enjoy discussing my books. There is cake too (but only if you bring it).

https://www.facebook.com/groups/1151907108277718

Made in the USA
Columbia, SC
06 February 2025

53377840R00136